Y0-AIM-916

Doria

Doria

Irene Parsons

1998
Galde Press, Inc.
Lakeville, Minnesota, U.S.A.

Doria
© Copyright 1998 by Irene Parsons
All rights reserved.
Printed in Canada
No part of this book may be used or reproduced in any manner whatsoever without written permission from the publishers except in the case of brief quotations embodied in critical articles and reviews.

First Edition
First Printing, 1998

Cover art by Mary Knudson Schulte

Library of Congress Cataloging-in-Publication Data
Parsons, Irene.
   Doria / Irene Parsons. — 1st ed.
     p. cm.
   ISBN 1–880090–73–2 (trade paperback)
   I. Title.
PS3566.A7715D6   1998
813'.54—dc21   98–6623
                                                                              CIP

Galde Press, Inc.
PO Box 460
Lakeville, Minnesota 55044–0460

Contents

Chapter 1	1
Chapter 2	7
Chapter 3	13
Chapter 4	21
Chapter 5	25
Chapter 6	33
Chapter 7	39
Chapter 8	49
Chapter 9	53
Chapter 10	61
Chapter 11	73
Chapter 12	81
Chapter 13	85
Chapter 14	97
Chapter 15	107
Chapter 16	117
Chapter 17	123
Chapter 18	129
Chapter 19	135
Chapter 20	143

Chapter 1

MAIA HAD ALMOST come to agree with T. S. Eliot. If April wasn't the cruelest month, it came in a close second.

She stared out the French doors opening onto the garden. The air was balmy—too warm for a Maine April. The yard made a mockery of the air, and it still looked like winter. Bare branches scratched at the sky, damp leaves clung along the bottom edge of the fence like a ragged brown ruffle, and dry grass sprawled every which way, as if it had been trampled in some mad dance. Maybe the dance of the demons which had tortured her mother these last gloomy months, Maia thought. Had they leapt and whirled and connived right there in her garden, how they would in turn offer pain, then ease, then hope, then pain again.

Maia shook her long, straight, blonde hair to clear the unholy vision. The neighbor's cat, black and white, stepped silently through the tangle of leaves, its eyes and ears alert to some prey out of Maia's line of vision.

She had stayed in her apartment across town until January. She had continued her work as curator of the small museum, bowing only to the necessity of taking long lunch hours in order to help her mother through the middle of the day. She made lunch, helped her with bathing, and tried to make a bit of chatter, to bring some outside world normalcy into the brittle facade of well-being in the house.

They both knew Helen's prognosis and its inevitable result. They just didn't talk about it. Maia thought one day that their exchanges about the weather, the price of butter, television programs, were skimming over the top of their feelings and fears like the fat from the vegetable soup she was making, leaving the meat, the values of their relationship, untouched.

Well, maybe they were both afraid, Maia thought, afraid of exploring what they had meant to each other, afraid of learning what they could have meant. Maia knew she had feared her mother's judgement ever since, when at eleven, she had confided shyly that she had reached a milestone of maturity. Helen had reacted with barely disguised distaste, leaving Maia feeling crushed and vaguely guilty. She was careful, after that, about sharing.

For her own part, she never asked the real reasons for the coolness between her parents before her father died when she was seven. Her mother had withdrawn from interest in Jack's business, his hobbies, his bed. Maia had tried to be part of their separate existences, and was almost relieved when, at Jack's sudden death in an auto accident, she didn't have to try anymore.

From then on, her mother had become even more aloof, living a lavish social life on Jack's generous insurance money. She redecorated the big house on Chestnut Street in authentic eighteenth-century grandeur. Maia was sent off to boarding school, then finishing school and college.

Helen had managed the early months of her own illness quite well. After the surgery, her part-time maid doubled as part-time practical nurse. Maia visited frequently and they developed a surface pattern of sociability.

But as the symptoms returned and deepened, and Helen became more uncomfortable and complaining, the maid resigned. Helen became irate with the visiting health-care people, and it had eventually become necessary for Maia to devote more and more time to her mother. She lived in her apartment as long as she could, but finally succumbed to the need to spend almost all her time in the big house. She made arrangements at the museum to share more and more of her duties with an assistant. She did not renew her apartment lease in December; instead she had put her things in storage and had moved "back home" with her mother.

Well, it was over now. Helen had fought the good fight, dragging her emaciated body through the long winter while Maia had done what she could—conferred with doctors, simmered watery soups, cajoled her mother to sip them, kept her mother's friends informed, and served them tea during their ever more rare visits.

And finally, she had acquiesced to her mother's last cry for release. She didn't think much about those moments. They were simply an extension of what she had been doing for months, a final gesture of comfort.

Maia shook her head again and looked around at the expanse of large eighteenth-century furniture. She could almost smell a heavy sweet scent from the dark, dense flowered wallpaper on the dining room walls. It seemed to crowd out the air. The suffocating sensation worked like a catalyst. Maia pushed out of her chair, moved quickly to the open French doors, and breathed deeply of the soft, darkening air.

"I've got to get out of here," she said aloud. "I can't stay in this house!"

It was the end of a series of long, long days. The early morning her mother died was a blur—the doctor's visit to sign the death certificate, his warm condolences, the people from the crematory, calls to distant cousins and friends. The phone had rung constantly, and Maia developed a set of words she repeated to each caller: "Yes, thank you. Yes, it was very hard. The memorial service will be Wednesday at 10:00 A.M. No, no burial service. No, there's nothing, but thank you."

Flowers came to the house, and pans of cakes and bowls of salad. She was alone. Her assistant from the museum offered to stay with her, but she refused. She wanted to be alone, to be at peace with herself as her mother was finally at peace.

She had got through the memorial service that morning rather well, she thought. She had felt composed, an almost unreal calmness. A number of people had come to the house afterward, where her mother's friends had made tea and served most of the donated food.

And now she was quite alone. Quite alone. Alone. Thirty-four years old, college degrees in art and history, some world travel, a few memories she couldn't quite forget, and a dead-end job in a small, stuffy museum. *Some résumé,* she thought. *Some kind of history. Some kind of life.*

The newspapers from the last hectic week were piled on the kitchen counter. Maia flicked through them, scattering them on the floor in a storm of newsprint, and found the ads. Employment opportunities, auctions, cars, trucks for sale; homes for sale, for rent. There weren't many homes for rent, and so the ad stood out:

> For lease, Doria, fine 1 BR secluded hilltop home on 5 wooded acres, on river and stream, 20 mi. from coast. 673-4267 Andy.

It sounded perfect. No traffic, no sirens, no salesmen. Maia knew there was a small inheritance from her mother that would come through before her savings ran out. She could get by for a year. She would take a leave or maybe quit her job at the museum. Just the thought of the musty relics, the panorama of the world's griefs and glories held motionless, the calculated effort to capture the past and make time stand still made Maia panic. She yanked open the kitchen door and clung to the frame as she gulped the warm, moist air.

Helen's cat, Sissy, slowly rose from her favorite spot by the heat register. Sissy seemed untouched by the loss of her mistress. She wrapped her tiger-striped body around Maia's ankles, her long tail slid up Maia's legs. To Maia it seemed the same soft, irresolute clinging as Helen's lingering over the past months.

"Scat Sissy! Get away! *Get away!*" She kicked out at the surprised cat, which backed off and snarled. What'll I do with that cat? I won't keep her—maybe the neighbors? The vet? Another final release?

She resolutely turned her thoughts from Sissy. She would take her miniature schnauzer, Kastor, with her. He would be the kind of company she needed—uncomplicated, undemanding willingness to accommodate to Maia's moods and needs. He would be equally ready to walk with her or snooze at her feet while she read or painted. And his sharp barking would announce any visitors to whatever escape she found.

Chapter 2

Andy Turrick caught the phone on the first ring. His voice was gruff and short. He seemed reluctant to show Doria to Maia.

"It's a pretty isolated spot. Except for a few…well… shacks, and a little general store at the foot of the hill, there are no other homes or businesses for miles. Hardly a house for a woman—you'd be alone?"

Maia assured him isolation was just what she wanted…needed. "I'm quite self-sufficient," she said almost defensively. "And for now I'm thinking only of the coming summer months, when it will be pleasant to be outside, and the roads will be open."

He picked her up the following Tuesday morning in an old dark-blue Buick. Maia thought his appearance was no more reassuring than his voice. His wiry red-gray hair hung in a tangled brush over his scowl. His gray eyes squinted sharply at her as if commenting unfavorably on her judgement. His nose had obviously been broken and took up permanent residence slightly off-center. And when he smiled a greeting, his thin lips revealed very white but crooked teeth. Maia had the brief sensation of viewing an example of "fractured art," a passing fad of the late fifties, in which none of the lines defining a figure met, but instead picked up some distance from where they left off, offering a form disconcertingly disconnected, as if being viewed in an antique mirror or a crazed, lacquered surface.

It was a cloudy day, with wisps of fog lingering in low areas and the sweet, rotting smell of sawmill wastes hanging heavily on the air. The graveled road to Doria meandered through the tree-covered coastal hills and along open fields. The farmhouses were connected with barns by miscellaneous buildings, like a series of afterthoughts which almost accidentally reached the conclusion of the barn.

They didn't talk much. Turrick seemed surly, displeased with Maia, with the whole prospect of showing Doria to her. So Maia was relieved when he slowed and turned sharply onto a narrow gravel drive. It led abruptly from the road up a steep hill and was edged by the thick rows of tall pines. A gate at the top had obviously been designed to discourage visitors but now hung in a broken pattern of wooden angles.

As the old Buick coughed and followed the steep curve of the drive, Maia caught her first glimpse of the house. She saw columns—many white columns—under a gently peaked roof. Broad cement steps on three sides led up to the roofed area. As Maia looked up at the structure, so different from the steep roofs and white siding of most Maine homes, a sudden impact of memory made her gasp.

"The Parthenon! Of course! Doria...Doric, tall pines...Greek cypress..." Andy looked over at her questioningly but made no comment.

After he parked the car, Maia got out immediately and started toward the house. She looked back at him, and he followed slowly. She moved along the stone path which was half-hidden by spreading grasses and dead pine needles. A tall, grotesque arrangement of tree stumps and rocks startled her as she came around a bush. She shivered and looked quickly at Andy.

"Kind of an odd structure, isn't it?" he asked drily.

"Yes, well, someone was having—creating—a work of art with the materials at hand." She smiled quickly at Andy to reassure him. "Let's go in."

The few rooms tucked back among the pillars at the center were like fresh air to Maia. White tile floors, thick white walls with deep window sills, a long living room with a wall of windows looking over a broad, tree-filled valley, a black marble fireplace. Maia appreciated the authenticity of the Greek Revival architecture. A large bedroom with glass doors opened onto a small lawn and the grove of pines. There was a large kitchen and spacious bath, cool with white marble.

Maia felt the claustrophobia of her mother's house slide away. She went back outside and wandered around the patio which wrapped the room on three sides. Andy followed at a distance, offering no information unless asked.

"Where are the lot boundaries?"

"Along the drive on the west, behind those big willows north of the house, down to the river on the south and along the little stream on the east."

"And there are five acres?"

"Thereabouts."

"Could we go down to the river?"

"Wouldn't advise it. Pretty slippery when those rocks and dead leaves are wet. It's quite a long way down—and steep."

Maia flared up. "You don't seem very enthusiastic! Why are you showing Doria if you don't want to rent it?"

After a few seconds, Andy looked directly at her and said shortly, "I just don't think it's the right place for you."

"How do you know what is the 'right place' for me? You don't even know me! I don't think it is very professional of you to pre-judge clients!"

"It's part of my job," he muttered, and walked to the car to wait while Maia walked through the house again. She was angry—and disappointed. She was set in her own mind that

Doria was what she needed now, and wanted some kind of confirmation from the only person around to reassure her. Well, I can do without it, and Andy Turrick can just do the rest of his job and write up the lease!

As she stopped on the stone path to look back at the house, its columns white against the low clouds, a slight breeze brought another wave of the cloying, sticky smell from the sawmill across the valley.

Chapter 3

Maia didn't have time to meditate on the cruelty of April. She spent its remaining weeks in an unaccustomed flurry of busy-ness. She arranged for a leave from the museum. Her more sensible self won over her recent inclination to quit altogether. "Maybe in six months I'll be glad to come back," she said to the flowers on the dining room wall.

She decided to simply lock up her mother's house and walk away. It would keep. Decisions about it and all it held could wait for another time. A neighbor offered to check on it and take care of the small yard. The neighbor even offered to take Sissy, although she hinted strongly that she thought

Maia ought to want her mother's cat. It was, after all, a living remembrance.

Maia arranged to take only minimal furniture, not wanting to clutter up that pristine house on the hill with mahogany Chippendale tables and tapestry-covered wingback chairs. She took a simple, white-painted kitchen table and two chairs, a box of food, dishes and pans, a reading chair and small floor lamp, a radio, her paints, nearly all her books, her bed, a few cotton shirts, skirts, sandals, and a heavy sweater.

Everything fit into a small rental trailer, including a few things she knew were inappropriate. Well, the wool wall hangings she had bought in Greece might be all right, although another comfortable chair would make more sense. She took the urn which had held her mother's ashes, before she buried them in the garden under the trampled grass, and a set of pale-green, sheer curtains. And of course Kastor her dog.

After she got it all together she hired a young man from the corner gas station to pull the trailer to Doria, to follow Maia's old Corvette along the dusty roads and help her unload it.

Andy had finally written up a six-month lease through his agency. The owner's name did not appear on the lease. He reluctantly relinquished the keys to her. She had found the intricate way back to Doria without quite knowing how she did it. She hadn't asked Andy for a review of directions, as she doubted he would have given them to her. He was, during their one subsequent meeting, absolutely stony faced. He gave her minimum information on the essential workings of the place—where the pump and electrical boxes were—and gave her a list of emergency numbers to call. Maia didn't notice his number at the bottom and would have sniffed if she had.

After her things were in place and the young man had raced down the steep drive with a squeal of brakes and wild lurch of the trailer at the bottom, total silence lay like a warm blanket over Doria. It was midafternoon on a warm early-spring day, and even the birds were apparently napping. Maia wondered if it was always so quiet here, or if the birds were holding back in judgement on the new tenant.

As Maia and Kastor walked toward where she guessed the stream ran along the east edge of the lot, she heard the faint sounds of water over rocks, a clean sparkling fresh sound. Maia decided it was a gentle welcome to her new home.

The stream, where it met the river, was choked with dead branches and leaves. She wondered if they were the residue from just one winter, or if many seasons had passed with no one clearing the stream. She wished she had asked Andy how long it had been since anyone had lived at Doria. The large, flat area on the riverbank was covered with long dead grass, twisted and flattened like the grass in her mother's lawn. Maia shivered and looked toward the broken wooden picnic table and blackened stones in a circle around an old fire ring. She decided she would fix up the table and make it a pleasant spot.

As she turned to go back to the house, a gray something moved between the trees and into the brush. Kastor growled and ran toward it. Maia knew it must be a cat—whose cat she couldn't imagine. *Maybe it comes with the territory,* she thought, and didn't like the idea.

The climb back up the hill toward the house was steep, and Maia recalled with a twinge of irritation that Andy had been right. But the month since they had first looked at Doria had been dry and warm, so the path was not slippery. But it released pungent odors of moisture and rotting leaves against Maia's feet.

A fork in the path took her toward the other end of the lot. As she pushed through a dense stand of evergreens, Kastor suddenly stopped and growled. Maia saw another small animal, this time yellow-striped, slip away through the bushes. Maia thought of Sissy. No, it couldn't be Sissy. Kastor hung back against her legs.

"It's all right, Kassie, just another cat. Where are they coming from?"

A bit farther through the trees she was surprised to find a small shed, completely hidden in the trees. *Why didn't Andy tell me about it?* she wondered. On further inspection, she decided it was hardly worth mentioning. It was small, perhaps eight by ten feet, and badly in need of repair—or, more likely, removal. Paint peeled from the window frames and the weathered shingle sides were warped and cracked.

Maia pushed at the door, but it didn't budge. She twisted the rusty knob harder, but it still didn't release the latch. Locked. *Why would anyone lock this wreck of a shack?* she wondered. *Someone must think it is worth keeping—or something inside it.* She wiped dust from one of the windowpanes and tried to look in, but the unreal late-afternoon twilight that sifted through the grime and cobwebs showed only indistinct objects stacked in a corner and what looked like an old blanket on the floor.

She finally gave up, pushed ineffectually at the door again, and looked for Kastor. He was busy sniffing around the other side of the shack. Maia sniffed too, at a strange animal odor she didn't even want to identify.

"C'mon, Kassie, I guess we aren't going to find out what this is all about today. Maybe I'll have to call Andy to find out what he knows, although he certainly didn't seem to want to tell me any more than he had to. Maybe he thought I would never find this building.

"Let's go back up to the house, finish unpacking, and find us some supper." They pushed through the dense undergrowth as they make their way back through the pines, up the grassy knoll, which was struggling against takeover by the poplar and rangy weeds extending from the surrounding groves. "We may have to get some goats to keep this little field open," Maia said to Kastor, who was leading the way, seeming already to know just where his supper was.

Maia looked up at the house, its white pillars gleaming in the clear light of a lowering sun, their tall shadows leaning against the walls of the house. An intense, painful moment of déjà vu made her stop and catch her breath. Suddenly she was back in Greece, looking up at the original fluted Doric columns, at the broken lines of the gently sloped roof where the Elgin marbles had once looked down on Athens, on the Plaka, on the glories that were Greece. With the view of the original Parthenon came the hurtful memories that went with it, the memories she had spent years trying to forget.

The trip to Greece when she was eighteen years old had been itself a monumental effort at forgetting. She felt a familiar stabbing pain in her chest. That baby boy. The tiny, black-haired bit of brand new person. That pink fist that had gripped her finger. The terrible emptiness when the nurse took the flannel-wrapped bundle, whom Maia, during the brief hour she'd held him, had named Peter, to his new parents. What was his name now? Where was he?

Helen had been unexpectedly calm when Maia had told her she was pregnant. She must surely have been surprised, because Maia had never shown much interest in boys. Maia was, in fact, pretty much a loner, with few close girl friends either. Maia knew her mother, quick, outspoken, and socially active in her widowhood, must sometimes have wondered that she had borne this quiet, self-contained child.

But Maia learned another side of her mother when she told her she was four months pregnant. Helen had inquired gently about the father, listened calmly as Maia briefly told her he was someone she had met at a freshman mixer at college, that he was handsome, charming, and absolutely not interested in marriage. Helen had been quiet for a few minutes while Maia clenched her teeth, her nails biting her palms, and studiously avoided looking at her. It had been a terrible moment, but no worse than the long three months she had wrestled alone with her problem.

The decision to put the child up for adoption had been agreed almost without discussion. Helen had been supportive and non-accusatory during the remaining months. There were no stormy scenes. Helen's friends seemed sweetly understanding and nonjudgmental. It was all very civilized. And Maia had kept her anguish to herself.

The baby had been born in a small hospital about a hundred miles from Pembroke. Maia had not met the adoptive parents. And in order to put the whole thing behind them, Helen and Maia spent two weeks in Greece the next April. It was a return to familiar haunts and memories for Helen, who had honeymooned there. It was, for Maia, an introduction to the actual sites of the mythological figures she'd found fascinating since childhood. The trip was also a return to her own very beginnings, as she had been conceived in an old hotel near the center of old Athens and named both for the month of May and for the nymph, Maia, mother of Hermes.

The scenes of the vitality and zest that had permeated classical Greek times gradually had reached through Maia's heavy mood and slowly melted some of her sadness. She and Helen walked through the Agora, the shopping mall of 2,500 years before; they spent evenings in taverns in the Plaka, the huddle of old stores and homes below the hill of the Parthenon, where riotous Greek dancing and toasting ended the evenings along with a few plates broken against a stone wall. And they trudged several times up to the Parthenon itself, letting the purity, the dignity, the sense of almost eternal beauty etch itself into their minds.

It was this vision superimposed on the columned house facing the sun above her that suddenly devastated Maia. Her mother was gone. The baby she had never known was gone, grown…how old? Sixteen? The pain of loss was a physical thing in her chest. And it suddenly struck her that she had sent them both away. "I'm alone because I sent them both away!"

Would she wish her mother back, to suffer again as she had suffered? Would she stand again with that pillow over the barely fluttering breath? No, she couldn't wish her back, but she experienced a physical pain to see her, to hear her voice.

And Peter. Did she wish she had kept him? She guessed she would never be sure, with all the unknowns of raising a child with no husband. But she still missed him; he was a part of her, wherever he was.

Maia was brought suddenly back to the present by Kastor, barking from the top of the hill. He was on the steps of the patio, calling for his supper. Maia breathed deeply and resumed her climb. *I have some healing to do,* she thought, *and I'm not sure Doria will make it easy. Maybe, as Andy said, this isn't the place for me.*

Chapter 4

IT WAS A LONG NIGHT. After Maia fed Kastor and put together a light supper from groceries she had brought from her mother's house, she wandered around the cool, sparse rooms, trying to feel at home. She hung the rough wool Greek arras on the living room wall. She moved her reading chair and lamp several times, trying to find the best early evening light. She scattered her books on the mantle and window sills to make the room look lived in. She mentally promised her mother's urn, sitting beside the fireplace, that she would keep it filled with the flowers she loved. Kastor followed her, his long-clawed paws tapping a nervous staccato on the white tile floors.

"I know—let's start ourselves a little 'welcome home' fire," she announced to him. His left ear twitched and he barked his acknowledgement of her brightening mood. As they stepped out the door and onto the path leading to the driveway, the weird sculpture of wood and stone loomed in front of her. Her heart skipped a beat, then began hammering in what seemed like double time. After a brief pause, she used her training as an art critic and made herself think what a contrast its grotesque unhumanness was to the classical human statues near the Parthenon. She pronounced her judgment of the artist: "Some sense of humor!" That calmed her fluttering pulse.

The air outside, heavy with evening dew, hung again with the sweet sawmill smell. Maia felt a brief wave of nausea.

She gathered a bit of kindling and several split logs from the small wood pile by the lot fence. As she turned to go back to the house, another cat, this one spotted black and white, disappeared behind the house. Kastor didn't try to confront this cat, but hung back against Maia's legs, almost making her stumble.

The fire caught easily and crackled cheerily in the black marble fireplace. Maia moved her chair again up close to the fire. She tuned her small radio to a Mozart symphony. Kastor curled at her feet, and she settled to read. But she couldn't seem to get back into the light novel. She had been reading it the night before her mother died. As she dozed, the fire died and the radio station went off the air. An hour later, she tensed as an inner alarm pulled her nerves taut. Her head jerked from the back of the chair. Was that Sissy scratching at her bedroom door again? Or was her mother calling? Did her mother need her? Usually the pills kept her mother sleeping during the night. Had she forgotten the pills? Her eyes flew open as the scratching at the window became more insistent. Kastor's head came up too, and he barked sharply as he and Maia both caught sight of the gray cat before it leaped into the darkness. Maia felt a familiar clutch of panic.

"It's just a cat! It's not Sissy—it's just another cat, Kastor," she assured the dog, more for her own comfort than for his. "I suppose they get hungry—and I suppose we look like a good bet for a handout. Let's go to bed. Tomorrow we'll look around the neighborhood and get our phone connected. Although I don't know who we will call—you and I are quite alone, Kastor. Well…there are always Mother's friends."

Maia drew small comfort from that thought because those friends, thoughtful and well meaning though they were, had not encouraged her to move to Doria. They were concerned about her safety, her emotional state, and her loneliness. They had pursed their lips and shaken their heads in disapproval. And that disapproval, of course, had only increased Maia's determination.

Chapter 5

AFTER A BRISK WALK down the drive the next morning, around the corner and along the asphalt road, Maia and Kastor approached the settlement below Doria. The cluster of shabby buildings lay in a haphazard clutter, as if they had tumbled down en masse and been stopped only by the black ribbon of asphalt. They filled the inside curve of that road with faded walls, peeling doorways, roofs missing shingles, and a gravel road which tied them all together into a desultory community.

Maia later learned that, although the buildings had obviously been there a long time, the residents had never organized themselves into an incorporated town with a formal name and identity. But the area had an unofficial identity. It was known as The Place. It had, through a process of metamorphosis, become a working, though modest, community. The Place included more than the general store Andy had mentioned. Or rather, the general store was more than general: it was universal. It offered essential groceries and an occasional pot of something hot; serve-yourself sandwich makings and a few tables at which to eat them; beer to be imbibed far into the night at the same tables; a serve-yourself gas pump; basic hardware; hunting and logging equipment; and clothing ranging from plastic baby pants to denim work clothes. The Place had everything.

Besides the general store, which occupied a series of connected, assorted, and mismatched buildings, The Place included a dozen small houses whose occupants hired out for lumbering and farming jobs, worked at the sawmill, clerked in surrounding towns, or hunted and fished between welfare checks. The Place was not prosperous, but it had worked out a level of comfort in its own stringent way.

Maia hung Kastor's leash over the corner of an unpainted bench in front of the store, told him to "Stay," and entered the general store. Her first impression was the aroma of spices, garlic, and rosemary. The next impression was an almost overwhelming clutter. Every kind of merchandise seemed staked, hung, piled, suspended, shelved, boxed, bolted, nailed, or otherwise packed under the low-ceilinged expanse. Supporting wooden posts interspersed the inventory, holding up a grimy, sagging ceiling that seemed inclined to relax with a gigantic sigh and put a decent cover over the panoramic confusion below.

It took a few minutes for Maia to adjust her eyes to the dim light inside. As she glanced around, she met the steady gaze of the man behind the register. He was short and muscular—maybe paunchy, Maia thought. A faded denim shirt strained at the buttons down the front of a bulging torso. A fringe of gray-brown hair circled a bald head, and a bushy brown mustache divided his round face. He nodded slightly and his lips under the mustache smiled—although his dark brown eyes did not. "Afternoon. Help you?"

"Well, I'm...just...I mainly want to...get acquainted. We...I...have rented Doria, and brought very few things with me..." As the man stared noncommittally, she realized he probably was not interested. "Do you carry...do you sell...groceries?" she finished lamely.

"In the back." Maia felt his eyes follow her as she picked her way among the counters stacked with clothing, housewares, tools, and all the paraphernalia deemed essential to twentieth-century living.

She found the grocery area tucked behind a tall bread rack holding unwrapped loaves. A few sagging shelves held rice, sugar, flour, oil and other basics necessary to life. A large black iron pot on a two-burner stove behind the counter sent up a billow of steam laden with garlic. A small refrigerated case displayed well-spiced sandwich meat, butter, milk, a wide jar of small, oily-looking black olives, and a block of crumbly white cheese.

The woman presiding in this dark nook was short and chubby verging on fat, with fair, kinky, blowsy hair and sharp blue eyes. She wore a faded black jersey pullover which stretched tautly over her breasts. She smiled broadly at Maia, revealing widely spaced, small, yellow teeth. The smile was followed by, "Yes, Ma'am?"

Maia glanced around uncertainly. "Well, I need milk…and could I get some of those olives? As I told the man up front, I mainly came down to get acquainted. I've rented Doria for…at least the summer…and I wanted to meet my neighbors." She smiled a small smile. *I do seem to be talking too much,* she thought.

The woman's smile faded. "Doria? Up on the hill? You living there?" Her eyes changed from a warm twinkle to a faintly accusatory expression.

After a slight pause, Maia said hesitantly, "Yes…" She wanted to ask, "Is it all right? Is something wrong?" Instead she added firmly, "I'm taking a break from my work. I plan to…do some painting…and writing…" Her voice trailed off. *Well, I will write some letters at least,* she told herself defensively.

"You alone up there?" The blue eyes were penetrating now.

"Yes…no…I have my dog. He's outside the store."

"Well, dearie, you may want more than a dog for a friend up there, off by yourself." Her mood seemed to change to one of practical warmth. "My name is Selena. My husband up front is Barnabas. Barnabas Frang. Barney, we call him. His bark's worse than his bite."

"Have you had this store very long?" Maia wondered if it was a recent acquisition and the Frangs hadn't had time to organize it, or if its claustrophobic clutter was theirs by choice.

"Oh, we been here forever! Don't it look like it?" She laughed. "We just carry a little bit of everything folks might want. We tell 'em if we ain't got it, they don't need it." Selena laughed a hearty guffaw at her own cleverness. "I bet…" She paused and seemed to change gears. "What's your name?"

"Maia…Maia Prescott."

"I bet, Maia…Maia? That's a different name! Anyways, Maia, I bet we'll have everything you're goin' to need—more than you'll ever need…" She stopped herself, paused, and continued. "Well, we have lots of most everything here."

"Well…do you have any fresh vegetables?"

Selena's confident smile faded. "Not just now. But in a month or so we will. Me and my daughter, Acantha, have a big garden. Soon's things are ready, we sell 'em right here. Canthy—we call her Canthy—she's not real keen on raising vegetables. You know young people, always wanting something they ain't got, or to be someplace where they ain't. But with a little encouragement, she works right along with me. She's in school now. She don't like school too much either."

Selena sighed heavily. "I tell you, Maia, raising children ain't all roses."

Maia nodded slightly and picked up the milk and olives. "Shall I pay up front?"

"Yeah, Barney takes care of the business end."

As he handed Maia her receipt, Barney's eyes were no warmer than they were before.

Several days passed pleasantly after Maia and Kastor first visited The Place. They explored the narrow, plunging stream and the broad river. Maia named it the River Lethe because it stirred up long forgotten memories of when her father had taken her fishing at a nearby stream—so long ago. Maia had looked over the neglected gardens and tried to decide how much effort to invest in them. And they had been back to the general store and found, except for the lack of fresh vegetables—which Maia soon discovered she could purchase at the nearby town of Delfson—that The Place offered enough variety of basic foods to actually sustain life. She found a cache of dried lentils and grains, a shelf of canned fruit, and a modest supply of crackers. And Selena periodically loaded up the bread rack with heavy, crusty, incomparably flavorful loaves of bread that she baked in one of the little houses nearby. The Place even carried Kastor's brand of dog food. Maia had to agree with Selena, with a wry smile, that if she couldn't find it at The Place, she probably didn't need it.

Maia and Kastor both enjoyed the exercise of the hike down the drive and along the little-traveled narrow asphalt road. They sometimes raced, Kastor free of his leash and easily outrunning Maia. Or they dawdled along the ditches, which were greening up with grasses and delicate elegant little plants that Maia knew would later become noxious weeds.

Eventually they met most of the inhabitants of The Place. They all looked at her, as Selena had, when they learned where she was living, but eventually seemed to forget it. Maia, more than once, wanted to ask, "Why do you look like that? What's wrong with Doria?" But the moment to ask always passed before she got the words out.

A couple of men were drinking at a little table in back late one afternoon when Maia hurried down for bread. Selena obviously felt she was performing a significant community service when she introduced them.

"Maia," she said, and paused to emphasize the importance of what was to follow, "Maia, this here is Hector Kadmos. And this is Phineas Solon. Heck and Phiny, they...uh...they're not married. And this here," gesturing proudly toward Maia as if she had personally produced her on the spot, "is Maia...Prescott."

Her words brought forth a raised eyebrow from Heck and a wink from Phiny, who solemnly lifted his beer bottle toward her. He caught Maia's eyes a long moment before the wink. Maia included them both in a brief smile, and nodded. She purposely did not look at Selena, whom she knew wanted to be acknowledged for what she probably thought was a turning point—for the better—in Maia's life. As she quickly walked to the front of the store, gripping the unwrapped loaf of bread under one arm, she felt the dark eyes of Hector and Phineas on her back.

Chapter 6

As May warmed toward June, all of Doria came alive. The hovering black, gnarled willows that had scraped and scratched ominously against the bedroom walls at night were suddenly graced with pale yellow tendrils sweeping toward the ground. The brittle gray rose brambles showed tender leaf buds along their thorny stems, promising a lacy green dress for the rough stone walls to which they clung. Sharp, deep green spears of wild strawberries opened tiny serrated leaves, covering the brown stems and crushed foliage of former summers. And wild grape reached tenacious tendrils along the weathered timber retaining walls.

The spread of long dead grass on the knoll below the patio was suddenly pierced with slender points of new grasses, mottling the brown expanse like a soldier's camouflage.

Maia, who had shared her mother's wide interest in flowers, nevertheless did not garden. She pulled away the dead leaves and stems to give the new sprouts of crocus and blue flags breathing space. She identified what plants she could, then decided to let Doria manage her own spring finery.

Instead, Maia got out her sketch pad and set up an easel on an old patio table. The valley toward the east was hung with scraps of fog like torn veiling over the greening tree tops. Solid pyramids of black-green pine stabbed through the pale green brush. One dead tree, bare branches angled like twisted bones, stood in black contrast with a stand of white birch trees. The sky was arched bright blue over all, with a few cumulus clouds puffing up over distant hills.

Maia was accustomed to the quiet of Doria, pierced with occasional bird calls and punctuated once in a while with a muffled roar from a car or truck on the road below. So she shook her head and cocked it to be sure of what she thought she had heard. A pipe! Unbelievably, the sound of a pipe or flute came softly up the hill! A thin strand of notes strung on the sunny air. Maia took a moment of sheer pleasure in the sound before she let herself wonder where it came from.

Actually she didn't have to wonder. She could tell it came from the copse of trees and bushes hiding the old shack. She hadn't gone back to it since that first day, figuring it was just a secret part of the scenery. She put down the charcoal she had been holding in preparation for a preliminary sketch. "Here, Kassie, come with me. Let's…let's see what—or who—is making music."

As they approached the shack, the notes stopped in the middle of a phrase, as if the music maker had stopped to listen. "Hal…lo—Hallo!" Maia's second call was firmer. Kastor growled but stayed close to her feet. When they came around the corner and looked into the door, now unlatched and pushed inward, they saw a young man sitting cross-legged on an old blanket on the floor. His fingers were still poised over the holes of the delicate instrument in his hands.

He looked up and grinned. *Why, he's just a boy,* Maia thought as she stepped through the door. They surveyed each other, motionless for a moment. "Who…who are you?" Maia asked. Kastor growled again and stayed in the doorway with her.

"Oh, I'm just…a…a traveler, I guess. Who are you?"

Maia was taken aback by his bluntness, figuring she was owed something of an apology for his uninvited presence instead of an accounting by her.

"Maia Prescott—I live her. I have rented Doria for the summer. This…building is on Doria grounds. You…you are trespassing, you know."

"Oh, I know you live here. I've seen you come and go—but I didn't know your name."

"You've seen me? How long have you been here?" Maia shuddered as she imagined being watched through the trees.

"Oh, just since yesterday. This time. But I've been here on and off for…months, I guess. I come and go a lot."

"Don't you have a home—a real home, I mean. I mean, is this your home?" Maia's eyes swept the interior of the shack, bathed in slanting sun rays, dimmed by the dust and cobwebs on the windows. Some small brown paper bags sat on a narrow shelf among a few cracked dishes. In the corner, a tightly rolled sleeping bag and other bundles were partly covered by a dark, ragged blanket. Next to them was a guitar, decorated with softly gleaming shell-like facings, and a strange long stick with something wound around it—a vine? A dirty brown backpack hung on a nail. And in the corner several bottles stood together, green and amber. A faint aroma of sour wine hung in the air.

Maia's eyes came back to the man-boy on the floor, whose wide gaze was still on her face. "Is…this your home?"

"As much as any place, I guess." He rose with a single, graceful push of his sandaled feet against the blanket beneath him. He was taller than Maia expected, and even slimmer. His eyes were large and dark and easily overwhelmed his narrow nose and full, almost petulant lips. The beginning of a beard shadowed his chin. But his hair held Maia's eyes. It was dark, thick, tightly curled over his forehead, but swept up on the sides in perfect, shining wing-like flares. *How does he keep it that way,* she asked herself incongruously. Then, *how does he live?* Aloud, "How do you live? I mean…eat…stay warm?"

"I seem to find enough to eat. And stay warm?" His eyelid moved slightly. A wink? "There are ways to stay warm."

"Well, I can't let you stay here. I think you should go home to your parents. How old are you?"

"Old enough, Miss Prescott,"—he said her name with exaggerated politeness—"to take care of myself. Been doing it for a long time now. My parents?" He laughed a hard dry laugh. "They don't much care. They have…other interests."

"But…but I can't let you stay here! What if…what if something happened to you? Someone from your home is surely looking for you. I feel responsible to get you back to your family."

Maia's heart was beginning to pound with panic and the realization that she didn't know what to do. She couldn't send this child-boy just packing. She could call the police, but she didn't want to cause… "What is your name?"

"Herm…Herman."

"Herman what?"

"Just Herman."

Maia didn't want to cause Herman any trouble with the law. Trespass was not, after all, a serious offense.

"Are you hungry?" The offer of food seemed a plausible and humane delaying tactic.

The big brown eyes lit up and the sensuous lips parted in a smile, revealing perfect teeth. "Ever see a boy who wasn't hungry?"

It was just the right thing to say. For a split second Maia thought of her own dark-haired boy who would be just about Herman's age. Could he be hungry now, someplace? Running? Scared?

Maia returned the smile and a bond was formed—or at least it was a recess in the interrogation. She turned, called Kastor, and suggested Herman come up to the patio for something to eat. *I'll not let him in the house,* she thought. She was almost ashamed of her defensive instincts. Just a hungry kid—on the lam—from someplace.

And after Herman had wolfed down half a loaf of bread, large chunk of cheese, a quart of milk, and an apple, she was defenseless against his request to at least spend a few more nights in the shack…"until I find someplace."

Chapter 7

MAIA WAS ALWAYS AWARE that the feral cats lurked in the trees, but as Herman strode down the hill after eating that day, the cats—the striped Sissy imposter, the lean gray one, and the huge black and white tom—bounded out of the dead grasses and tried to twine themselves around his moving legs. Maia suppressed a shudder. She could feel them around her own legs.

The impression was strong enough to take her thoughts from the receding figure to the real Sissy, and how that cat had rubbed against her ankles in the house on Chestnut Street the day of her mother's memorial service. And standing in the bright sun, she thought again of her mother, lying in the darkened, dead-smelling room. Maia stood again with the pillow in her hand, looking down at her mother's emaciated face, at the half-closed eyes. She heard the rasping breath. Her heart lurched again with the sickening awareness of her mother's pain and desperate pleading. And her stomach turned sour with guilt.

Instead of fading with time, Maia's unease was becoming sharper. Her good sense told her that what was done, was done. There had been no legal inquiry about the cause of death. She must learn to be thankful for that, at least, and leave it behind. She had been sure this beautiful remote spot would help her find peace. And during the days, she was usually successful. She kept busy with creative cooking, spicing the bare necessities from The Place with herbs she found growing wild in the garden—basil, oregano, fennel, chives. She made charcoal sketches of scenes she could see in all directions from the patio, and had even done a small landscape in watercolors. The long walks she took with Kastor took them exploring the local roads and lanes. And there were always the shopping expeditions to The Place and to Delfson for fresh produce.

But the nights were long and unsettling. When the soft spring dusk fell over Doria and the surrounding hills, Maia and Kastor retreated to the house. While the evenings were still cool, a fireplace was a comforting third presence. But when it became too warm for a fire, Maia struggled to open long-unused windows to let in cooling breezes. She haunted the classical music station on her radio. After reading and re-reading the books she had brought with her, she read the few books she found appealing on the battered bookshelf at The Place. She even resorted to trying to write poetry in an effort to sort out her conflicting emotions about her parents—and herself.

Eventually, though, she had to go to bed every night. The ever-present hilltop breezes kept the willows brushing against the bedroom walls. Night insects strummed and thumped the window screens in their own erratic, unscored, nightlong symphonies, with background moaning from the wind in the pines. The gray cat often leapt silently onto the window ledge and gazed in on her, or gently scratched at the screen. Maia willed herself to accept these night noises as part of the solitude she had sought.

But still she did not sleep. She relived, over and over, the hour she had held Peter, felt the tiny flexibility of his slight weight on her arm, wrapped in the white fuzzy blanket; smelled again the new baby sweetness; touched the downy blackness of his hair, the warm pink scalp beneath. She could feel the diminutive fingers around her own, hear the gentle breathing. She watched again the pink tranquil face as he slept, and willed again that the eyes would open so she could see him awake. And they had opened, for one long, thoughtful look directly into her own eyes. Maia still recalled that short time as the most real, the most significant, of her whole life. How could she have let it go?

That hour was her first and final time with Peter. When her mother entered the hospital room just then, a forced optimism in her smile, Maia had asked hesitantly if there was any way she could keep Peter. Helen had briskly counted the reasons. They had been through them all many times: Maia was scarcely more than a child herself. She was in no financial position to raise a child. She must finish her education. The child would be better off with both a father and a mother. And besides, "the papers are signed." Maia knew she would never forget the finality of those words. How could a wisp of paper have dominion over this baby—her baby!

But the nurse had come in, smiled sadly at Maia, and lifted Peter from her arms. Helen did not look at the baby. As the door shut after them with a soft whisper, Maia's eyes locked briefly with her mother's, closing the episode. It was the end of Peter in Maia's life.

Somehow her own life went on. During those sleepless nights at Doria, Maia relived the following years behind closed eyes. There was the trip to Greece with her mother. Then she had plunged into college classes, excelling in the areas of art and history because she loved them. She had drawn away from her mother during those years but had not made any close friends to fill the gap. She was most happy alone, with a sketch pad or box of watercolors out in some wild, quiet place. Subsequent jobs at art museums fit well into her mode of life—solitude, introspection, and the beauty of nature.

It was only as her mother's illness progressed that she had re-entered the life her mother had built, but only at the point where it was itself disintegrating. She took comfort from the fact that she had done her best to make her mother comfortable. She had resisted her own desire and need for a final chance to confront Helen over the decision to give up Peter. She knew it would do no good and would cause her mother pain, of which, God knew, she was having enough.

But Maia had wanted desperately to share her memories, still as fresh as they were sixteen years ago, with the only person in the world with whom she could share them. And now her mother was gone too. And again the fearful moment with the pillow would fill her being with horror. And again the blackness would come, and the memories would stop. Right there. Then again the unease she felt about Doria would take over: Andy's reluctance to rent it to her; the suspicious speculation of the residents of The Place; the feral cats slipping in and out of the trees, as if they, not she, were the rightful residents; the sticky, rotting aroma drifting over the valley; the feeling Doria had been unoccupied for a long time. Why? And, of course, the shack, and now Herman. What should she do about Herman?

Once she even felt so unsure of herself, so threatened by forces she couldn't name, much less understand, that she was tempted to call Andy Turrick and ask him why he had said that Doria wasn't the place for her. What did he know about Doria? And why didn't he tell her all about it, including the shack in the woods? Did he know about the shack? But her nighttime decision to call Andy, which had given her relief from her tension so that she had finally slept, evaporated with the morning mists, and she again put him out of her mind.

Herman stayed on in the shack, and the "few nights" he requested stretched on through the end of May and into June. Maia wasn't sure how she felt about him. At times, when he wolfed down bread, meat, and milk on her patio, his thin frame folded over the rickety table, she felt a maternal urge so strong it almost brought tears. He could so easily be Peter—couldn't he? His smile would flash brilliant thanks and his eyes crinkled with pleasure as he finished his milk and wiped his mouth on his wrist. And Maia melted.

He willingly answered Maia's questions about the Doria gardens, which were emerging in soft-colored patches like those on the quilt her grandmother had made and given her years before. Herman had a surprisingly vast knowledge of the trees and flowers opening in the June sun. These times were very pleasant for Maia. She soaked up the information about plants that he offered along with bits of fascinating mystical lore, variations on the myths she had loved for years, but long forgotten, and uses of herbs practiced by the ancient gods. Maia let herself be immersed in Herman's tales, patching in her own extensive knowledge of mythology and antiquity. But she would be brought back to reality occasionally when she brought snippets of plants to learn more about them, and lean near Herman to tuck the leaves or flowers into a jar on the table. Then she always smelled the same pungent, sour odor she had noticed when she first discovered him in the shack. She thought it must be some kind of wine, and wanted to mention it—he was so young; she wouldn't want her Peter to drink it—but she hesitated. His warm good humor could cut off abruptly, either for no reason Maia could figure, or always and surely when she gently asked about his family, his early years, or even about his relationship with The Place and how he spent his time. To ask about his drinking would again cut off the sunshine he spread.

His lips would thin to a straight line, and his eyes would harden to narrow black slits. He would push the kitchen chair sharply from the table against the stone patio, the slim wooden legs almost splintering before his angry thrust. Without looking at her again, or speaking, he would stride off down the hill, his thin jeans-clad legs slashing against the lengthening grass. At those times, the cats kept their distance, eyeing him furtively from among the trees.

His mood changes kept Maia off balance and more than once brought her to the point of demanding he move out of the shack at once. But he had an uncanny sense of just how much and when he could safely irritate her, and knew just when to flash that smile and say something conciliatory, something to make her laugh. She always weakened, but the half-wink which often accompanied the smile told her she was being manipulated.

Those were the nights she would lie awaken and decide firmly the very next day she would send him packing, only to catch her breath with pleasure on hearing the sweet sounds of his guitar or flute lilting up the sunny hill the next morning. Her irresolution was compounded by Herman's frequent and always unpleasant absences. About the time she had determined to forbid him use of the shack, to find another home, go back to school, anything to settle him away from her, he would suddenly be gone. No flute melodies filled the mornings—no guitar strumming floated on the evening air. After a day or so, Maia would wander down to the shack to find it as locked, empty, and unknowable as the first day she had found it.

Other times, when she felt they were becoming good friends, with trust building between them, she would relax with the sureness that he would confide in her, let her into his life so she could help him. And again, he would be gone, sometimes for many days. Maia would wander the house and yard, aimlessly straightening books, cutting a few greens or white roses for her mother's funeral urn, forgetting to eat, and tossing through endless nights, wondering where he was, determining again that she would end the relationship, only to feel indescribable elation at his return.

Maia was irritated at her own irresolution. It wasn't like her. She had always known her own mind, modest as its aims had been. And she wondered too why she was too reticent to mention Herman at The Place. Surely Barney and Selena knew about him. He likely got his wine from them. Maia guessed they didn't demand I.D. cards. She figured too that Herman was probably the reason they all looked so skeptical when she said she was living at Doria. What else could it be? She supposed it wasn't odd that they didn't mention him; she certainly wasn't on chatty terms with anyone there. And so she struggled alone with what to do with her uninvited guest.

Chapter 8

As she turned from watching Herman go down the hill one cloudy afternoon, Maia thought she saw something moving in the pines near the driveway. It was so fleeting, she wasn't sure she had even seen anything at all in the murky, dusky green shadows. But she knew if she had seen something, it was larger than a cat. She stared at the place a long time, her heart thumping painfully. She finally made herself move toward the dark place in the trees across the parking area. Her footsteps on the gravel crackled as she approached. As she neared the trees, a man's voice proceeded from the shadows.

"All right, you caught me! I give up!" Andy Turrick stepped away from the drifts of dry pine needles crunching under his feet and onto the drive. His crooked teeth grinned an awkward apology. Maia blinked in surprise. Had she conjured him up with her thought of calling him? But his approach, and his outstretched hand, assured her he was not an apparition.

"What…what in the world are you doing?" Maia's voice cracked with surprise and near outrage. She ignored the proffered hand.

"I'm sorry, Miss Prescott—Maia—I didn't mean to frighten you. I didn't mean for you to even see me."

Maia stared at him coldly. "Obviously. Or you wouldn't be skulking in the shadows! Where is your car? What do you want?" She kept an edge on her voice, even though she was, after her initial shock, slightly relieved to see him.

"Miss Prescott—can I call you Maia?"

She nodded almost imperceptibly. "You already have," she said drily.

"Maia, I've been worried about you. I thought you might call on me for an emergency. Did you see my name at the bottom of the list I gave you? Of course, I hope you haven't had an emergency," he added hastily, "have you?" He looked over her shoulder to where Herman had disappeared.

"No, I didn't see your name. And, no, I haven't had an emergency. Did you hope I would? Why were you worried about me?"

Before Andy could answer, she threw out the question which had kept her awake nights. "Is there a particular reason you worried about me here at Doria? Is there something about this place you haven't told me? And why didn't you?" She stared accusingly at Turrick, who shifted from one foot to the other.

"No...no...there's nothing about Doria."

"Well, did you know about the shack?"

"The shack? That little building down in the trees?" He hesitated a moment. "Sure, I knew about it. I don't handle property without investigating it thoroughly."

"Well, why didn't you tell me about it?"

"I just didn't even think about it. It's just an old wreck of a building—nothing to do with your living in the house. I never thought you'd even find it. When did you find it?"

"The first day I moved in! It upset me that you weren't totally honest."

"Honest! That's got nothing to do with honesty! I just didn't think it was a significant item!"

"What else haven't you told me about? And why are you here anyway?"

"No reason. Nothing. I just happened to be out this way, on an appraisal, and thought I'd see how you were doing."

"From the pine trees? Hiding in the shadows? Couldn't you just come right out and ask?"

"Well, I saw you had company..." He paused, waiting for her to elaborate.

Maia didn't. She had decided not to discuss Herman with Andy. She could determine what was "significant," too. This man made her angry!

"Yes, well, you can see I'm fine. If you think of any more secret information about Doria, don't hesitate to let me know!" She turned to stride into the house.

Turrick stared after her for a moment, then turned to walk slowly down the driveway. Maia watched him from the living room window and saw her main hope of feeling more comfortable about herself at Doria disappear behind the pines. He hadn't been open about the shack. He must know about Herman, too, but chose not to say anything. What else was he hiding? Why was he concerned? Why did he think she might have an "emergency"?

Chapter 9

Andy Turrick's visit, instead of easing Maia's mind, simply made her angry. She was now determined to make a comfortable summer for herself here at Doria without his help or interference. She let herself become even more protective of and attached to Herman. He became an avenue of re-entry into a world without guilt.

Slowly, as they spent more and more time together between his absences, as Maia watched with pleasure as he ate meals on the patio, as she laughed at his quirky humor and learned to ride out his moods, she had a sense of working out from under a heavy load, of doing an easy penance, erasing her past sins of giving Peter up for adoption and for the ultimate guilt-laden occasion of her mother's death.

Through working out this relationship, she thought she might help Herman rejoin the safer and more secure world she felt a sixteen-year-old needed. Surely the one he now inhabited seemed neither safe nor secure. And always, in the back of her mind, she felt she was doing it all for Peter, whom she had known for just one hour, but whom she had carried in her heart for sixteen years.

She began searching Herman's face for signs of a resemblance to herself, and to Tim, Peter's almost forgotten father. But that magnificent head of black curls and the lighter wings sweeping over Herman's ears seemed not related to her own stick-straight blond hair. Tim's hair? She remembered the stiff brush of worn upholstery against her bare arms, the discomfort of her twisted position below Tim's weight. She could still smell stale cigarette smoke and a faint odor of gasoline, dust, and oil, and hear the strains of dance music through the open car window. But Tim's hair? She couldn't remember.

Moving down, past the smooth, fair forehead, Maia decided Herman's silky, straight, black brows were like neither her own gently arched brows nor like Tim's wiry rough ones. And his brown eyes were his own, inherited from no one. She studied his nose. Maybe Herman's was straight and narrow, much like her own.

That quick, brilliant smile, Maia thought, could easily have come from Tim. It had been Tim's grin, that flashed perfect, even teeth and reached up to crinkle around his brown eyes, which had first caught Maia's eye, then her will power, as he had gently led her from the college dance nearly seventeen years ago and into the back seat of his old car. But she did not want to dwell on Tim or that night, even though a resemblance between Herman and Tim would partially confirm her own wishful thinking.

And so Herman gradually became Peter. Maia let herself luxuriate in the delusion that fate had dealt her a second hand, and that hand held a future for her and her son. Herman seemed to be warming to her, trusting her, and, Maia wanted to believe, loving her.

But when her tongue slipped one day and she called him Peter, Herman backed off. He stood tall in his ragged jeans and faded T-shirt.

"I am Herman, no one else."

And he stalked off down the hill. She heard the door of the shack slam through the trees.

One warm June morning, Kastor and Maia took the path to the river. She carried work gloves and a few tools, planning to clear the branches from the mouth of the stream and repair the picnic table. About halfway down, they heard splashing, and, between the fresh green leaves, saw someone swimming. Maia held Kastor's collar as they edged closer. It was Herman, swimming strongly from the other side of the river, which was high with spring rains and snow melt. Maia still hesitated, not wanting to walk on down and embarrass the boy, whose clothes lay on a rock, and not wanting to retreat and make noise in the underbrush. So she and Kastor watched Herman rise slim and tan from the water. Maia took pleasure in the straight young arms, the broad shoulders emphasizing the slender waist and hips, the lithe thighs. Water drops sparkled on the smooth skin and light seemed to radiate around him. *He looks like a Greek god,* was Maia's fleeting thought. And, as the first time she had seen him, his hair caught her attention. The black curls, flattened by the water, covered his head. As she watched, Herman moved his hands up and over his ears, pushing the dark mass away from his face. The hair, shining with water, swept high and smooth into the familiar wings.

The shadow Maia had noticed last month on his chin was becoming a dense, curly beard. It made him look older—a bit secretive. Maia stared at the easy grace and dignity Herman seemed able to display in spite of his tattered clothes—like a man used to walking—"a traveler," he had told Maia. The Greek god imagery struck her again. She watched as he picked up his clothes from a rock, pulled on his jeans, and threw his shirt over his shoulder as he started up the hill on another path, carrying his walking stick.

Suddenly it flashed through her mind. *Hermes! He...he looks like...Hermes! Hermes, son of...Maia.* For a minute her mind refused to work. The thought was too...ridiculous! Unconsciously she looked for Herman's shoes—looked for the winged sandals. But Herman had disappeared into the foliage and was gone.

Was this the mystery of Doria, that it was...haunted by history? Haunted by some strange projection of ancient Greece into the twentieth century? Was this why Andy Turrick seemed concerned for her? Didn't want her here? What had that red-gray-haired real estate agent to do with Greece and ghosts and young gods?

Maia slowly retreated up the path toward the house. She watched as the morning sun caught the white marble pillars in a grid of light and shadow against the brilliant blue sky above. *Colors of the Greek flag* slid through Maia's mind. And she thought about Herm...Herman, his elegant flute playing, his shell-faced guitar—a lyre? His strange walking stick, the stick with the vines wound around it. Vines? Or a snake? And his name: Herman—Hermes. First he was Herman, then Peter, then...Hermes?

What was there about this place that was taking her from the reality of her ordinary, even mundane existence, into this otherworld nightmare of mixed identities? Who was she, herself, then? Was she, in her love of solitude, her unease in crowds and the noise of the city, was she actually an alien from centuries past, thrust ahead in time? Or was she still Maia Prescott, museum curator, sometime artist? Or was she simply Maia, minor goddess, mother of Hermes, the bad boy of the Golden Age? Was her conception in that primitive little hotel deep in the Plaka of Athens a mark on her, to keep her forever tied to that murky if glorious age?

Suddenly she grasped at a tree trunk, leaned over, and was violently ill. Kastor stood quietly and watched as Maia retched and clung weakly to the rough bark. But when she let loose of his collar, he barked once, high and sharply, and for the first time since they had come to Doria, ran off through the trees. Maia called weakly, but he didn't come back. She wiped the vomit from her mouth on the hem of her blouse, swallowed the sour taste, and made her way back to the house. The bright June morning had turned gloomy with her sense that she had somehow lost her way.

Kastor did not return. Maia, confused and exhausted, called often and as loud as she could, walking around the house and down the hill through the tangle of weeds and vines. She didn't, however, go to the shack. Kastor had never seemed drawn to Herman, and she was fearful she would see him. She had no idea of how she would—or ever could—face him, after the trick her mind had played on her down by the river.

She didn't know what to do with herself, how to pass the day. She looked at her sketches and tried to choose one from which to work toward a finished picture. But they all looked stilted and amateurish. She tried reading one of the light romances she had found at The Place, but the characters seemed static, their worries and problems quite mundane. She couldn't make herself care about what they did or how they extricated themselves from silly, sticky situations that, Maia thought, they should have been able to avoid.

She finally made a supper that she was unable to eat, and, after calling for Kastor one more time, went to bed. She thought she had heard him bark once, far down the hill and deep in the trees, but he didn't come back. It was almost dark; Maia decided to wait until morning to look for him. In bed, she tossed on the slim foam mattress as she turned her own problems over and over in her mind.

What was her problem, exactly? That she seemed to have been born again after 2,500 years. And that she had a Greek god for a son. If she weren't so tense and half sick to her stomach, she would have laughed aloud.

Could she have avoided her situation? How? And did she even want to extricate herself from it? She had to admit she had never before felt so alive, so involved with another person, so...needed. Another thought, which she would hardly let herself acknowledge, kept tingling at the edges of her mind: the sight of Herman's strong young body at the river had excited an unfamiliar urge, the kind of urge she had been sure she would never feel again. Was this an unnatural inclination? Another thing for which she would have to atone? Her mind still in turmoil, Maia drifted off to a dreamless sleep, unaware that the gray cat sat at the window and watched her all through the night.

Chapter 10

MAIA WOKE with the sour taste of yesterday's turmoil still in her mouth. She lay quietly in bed staring at the sun slanting across the patio. It seemed so clean, so clear cut, so untouched by human confusion. Her own confusions sifted slowly back into her mind. At first she thought she must have dreamed them—the walk to the river, the boy-man rising from the water, the moment of transfiguration, her own interpretation of the apparition. Maybe it was a dream. Yes, it must have been a very lifelike dream.

"Kastor...Kassie?" But Kastor did not bound from his accustomed place at the foot of the bed to her side for his morning head ruffling. "Kassie?" Maia called once more, trying to push back the growing realization that it had not been a dream—a bad dream. Kastor was gone. The rest of the dream must have been real, too.

In spite of her drugged sleep, Maia felt energetic. She purposefully shook off the thought of Herman. She knew she had to find Kastor. And she knew she had to talk with someone—anyone—about this place, this Doria, where she had hoped to find peace and relief from her troubled mental state, but which had only given her more cause to mistrust her own judgment.

She showered and, for the first time in weeks, put on makeup, mascara, and a touch of lipstick. It was a thin armor of color for her foray into the unknown. After a cup of tea and a piece of toast, she set out in the direction from which she thought she had heard Kastor's bark last evening. She had not explored the area before, and found it had no paths and was an almost impassable tangle of wild grape vines, tall weeds, fallen trees, and brush. She struggled for several yards, tearing her shirt and turning her ankle painfully on the rocks and rough terrain before finally giving up. She stared ahead into the leafy green dusk of the woods and couldn't believe Kastor would have run into it.

"I must have imagined his bark came from here," she murmured to the bushes. "Maybe he didn't bark at all. I'm getting so mixed up I don't even know what I've heard!" And she turned to stumble back toward the semi-cleared knoll below the house. *If I am Maia, minor Greek goddess,* she thought ruefully, *I'm not carrying my goddesshood with much dignity!* Just then the yellow-striped cat turned a yellow eye on Maia as he slipped in front of her and away through the trees.

Keenly feeling Kastor's absence, she limped down the driveway and turned onto the road toward The Place. The day was flawless—bright sun, a few white clouds, slight breezes wafting a bouquet of aromas from innumerable budding and blooming trees, bushes, and plants. *Even the weeds smell good today,* she thought. The heavy scent from the sawmills was surprisingly, and thankfully, absent. It was a perfect day. *J. R. Lowell knew whereof he wrote! I should be happy to be alive and healthy on a day like this,* she firmly told herself.

And for a while she let herself be immersed in the beauty presented on the palette of the day. She slowed her walk and breathed deeply of the fragrance on the air. The birds were whistling their own airborne pleasure. Her artist's sense made her aware of the myriad greens of the foliage and the crooked black lines of the trees dissecting it. She watched her sandals step on the leafy shadows as they lay a border of gray lace along the road edge.

Even the mismatched buildings of The Place, wrapped unevenly in the curve of the road, took on a fresh look. *It's almost quaint,* Maia thought, which was a far cry from her former impression. She looked with new interest at the broken roof angles, the piebald walls, odd-shaped windows and doors of many sizes and colors. *I should paint it,* she thought suddenly. I could set up my easel back here, off the road, and catch that morning sun and the dark shadows. The Place will be my first oil painting at Doria! She began planning placements on the canvas, color densities, techniques, and overall impression, and felt a surge of satisfaction at making a firm commitment to herself, almost the first she had made since her arrival at Doria.

A car backed abruptly from the front of the general store and pulled away in a spurt of gravel and dust as Maia approached, spoiling the idyllic village view she had envisioned. As the cloud of dust cleared, it revealed the peeling paint, the broken cement steps, rusting tin roofs, and cracked windows. It was every day at The Place again. And with that onset of reality, Maia's brief joy in the day was spent. Kastor was still gone. He hadn't come racing down the drive or along the road after her. He hadn't been in the meadow across the road. He wasn't waiting in his spot by the unpainted bench in front of the general store.

And Maia had now to decide just how to initiate an inquiry to learn what she wanted to know about Doria. She regretted that she had been so reclusive, going down to The Place only for needed groceries and spending so little time there.

She needn't have worried. Selena seemed poised for conversation behind the food counter. There was no one else in the store; even Barney was absent from his usual reign behind the cash register. Maia pulled out a chair from the flimsy round table and sat down. "How about…" she paused, not knowing what she wanted, not wanting to even think about it. She spotted the full coffee pot. "A cup of coffee. Black."

Selena smiled broadly. "Sure, Mmm…Maia. Just can't get used to that name! Here you are." And she came from behind the counter, her ample bulk swaying from side to side, her heelless slippers slapping the grimy linoleum floor. "You're up early this morning, ain't you, Maia?"

Maia sipped the bitter black brew and nodded. "I…well, Kastor ran away last night. He's never done that before… and I can't find him."

Selena's usually open face closed for a moment, her smile faded, and her eyes slid toward the back door. "Oh. Oh, that's too bad. Maybe…maybe he'll come back."

"Well, I hope so. He's been my best friend since we moved to Doria—even before, I guess. I don't suppose you've seen him this morning?"

"No…no, I ain't seen him today. But it's nice for you to take time now to sit awhile." Selena gave Maia a look of slight accusation. "Seems like we don't know you very well."

"It's just that I've had a lot to think about, and needed to be alone."

"You ain't had…no visitors…at all?" Selena watched her closely.

Maia decided to ignore the question and plunge right into the other reason for her visit. "Selena, what do you know about Doria?"

Selena interpreted the question as an invitation to join Maia. She dropped her generous body onto one of the other chairs, which creaked in protest. "What do I know about

Doria?" she asked rhetorically. "Well, to start with, it's been there, oh, fifteen…eighteen years."

"Who built it?"

"Oh, it was some fellow from the city—an artist fellow—I think he did statues. He never spent much time here at The Place either." Again the accusing glance. "We all thought it was a kinda funny looking house, what we could see. He never invited any of us up there…either." Maia stared at her coffee cup. She didn't have to see Selena's look.

"Did he live there very long? Did he live there alone?"

"Well, let me see…seems to me he was up there about…oh, maybe ten years. Most of the time alone, but he had another fellow…from the city, too, I guess, anyways, not from around here…to help him put in his gardens. The gardener fellow came on and off for quite a few years. They had a lot of clearing to do; that was quite a thick forest up there."

"Yes, I know what's left is thick. I tried to find Kastor…"

"You went…into those woods?" Selena seemed suddenly tense.

"Yes, but not very far. Why?"

"Oh, it just don't seem like a woman would want to go thrashing around in them brambles."

"Well, I didn't want to, and I don't think Kastor did either. I didn't go in very far. I…I just don't know where he could be." Maia's voice broke as it hit home again that the dog was really gone.

Selena didn't seem to want to talk much about Kastor. "Anyways, it seemed like the gardener disappeared. We knew the police was up there askin' questions—state police, not our own sheriff, else we'd know a lot more about what went on. That was maybe four, five years ago. Then soon after, the owner…let's see…Phil…no, Philo Thad…Thad-something, never quite got it straight. That Doria seems to draw the odd names, Maia!" and Selena showed her gap-tooth smile to show there was no meanness intended. "Anyways, he left too, ain't been nobody livin' in Doria since then."

Maia stared at her cup. Phil Thad-something…Thaddeus? Thaddaios? Greek. Quite Greek—and a sculptor. *Well, that explains the architecture and, in a twisted way, that strange figure by the front door. I wonder if he started out in Athens—the Plaka—too. Wonder who he thought he was? Phidias? His sculpture at Doria is a far cry from Phidias' Athena.* She tried to remember if she had seen items in the art journals or local papers about a Philo Thad-something. Maia's wandering thoughts were interrupted by a discreet cough from Selena. Maia shook her head and tried to remember what was last said. "The…gardener…they never found where the gardener went?"

"Nope, guess he just left…with no forward address. Good way to do if you wanna get lost."

Maia couldn't quarrel with that. She thought of the Doria gardens, which must have been glorious before the years of neglect. Now they were a wilderness of rotting timbers, broken stone steps, drifts of dead pine needles, wild grape and rose brambles covering all. *A sad legacy,* she thought. *Nothing is forever, neither gardens nor gardeners.*

"Where did Philo Thad-something go?"

Selena shrugged. "He never left no forward address neither…leastways not with me!" She laughed shortly. "We never knew him when he was here. Sure never knew him after he was gone! Just packed up and left. S'pose he still owns Doria. There was a 'for rent' sign by the drive for a year or so, then I guess he just gave up. How'd you happen to land up there?" Selena asked abruptly.

"There was an ad in the paper. A 'for rent' ad. It seemed just right for me. But now…" Her voice trailed off.

Selena looked sharply at her. "What's the matter with now?"

Maia clenched her teeth and plunged ahead with the hardest question. "Do you know…Herman?"

Selena's face assumed a satisfied look. "I figured you'd get to Herman. Do you know Herman?" she asked mischievously.

Maia didn't smile, just repeated her question.

"Well, sure I know Herman. Everybody in The Place knows Herman. Fact is, some of us knows him a little too well—or he knows us too well."

"What do you know about him?"

"Well, I know he ain't been payin' much rent," and one eyelid dropped in the suggestion of a wink.

"You knew he was living on Doria grounds, and you never told me?"

"Well, you never asked me! Never hardly talked to me before." Selena look aggrieved. "Anyways, he ain't there much, just off and on."

"I know. Where does he go when he's not home—I mean, at Doria?"

"Lord knows, I don't. 'Spect he's got business."

"Business! That...child? What business could he have? He ought to be in school, growing up, learning a profession or a trade!" Maia hadn't meant to reveal this much of her feelings. She stopped speaking abruptly.

Selena put a rough hand out to pat Maia's hand. "You don't have to worry about Herman. Oh no. Herman is quite growed up already. And he's got a prof..." she stopped.

Maia studied Selena's face. "What do you mean 'got a profession?' What does he do when he's not...eating lunch at my house?" she asked with beginning anger in her voice.

Selena backed off with a dignified reserve. "I don't know. I didn't say he had a profession or anything. I don't know what he does."

"Well, what did you mean, he knows some people here 'too well'?"

Selena's new dignity dissolved into pathos. She swallowed hard and put a hand with red-cracked knuckles against a fat but sagging cheek. She suddenly looked defeated. "I don't mess in people's lives. I mean, it's not my business how people run their affairs. But sometimes...if they mess in my life..."

"Mess in your life?" Maia leaned forward, the perspiration standing on her upper lip.

Selena looked toward the front of the store as if to assure herself that no one—maybe Barney—was coming. "It's Canthy…Herman's been…well…messing with Canthy. I told you she's always looking for something exciting, don't like school, don't like raising vegetables. Well, she found something exciting. She found Herman."

Maia looked long and deep into Selena's small blue eyes, suddenly hurt and vulnerable. "Found Herman? How? You mean…?"

"You know what I mean! They found each other, I guess…and now…and…well, Barney and me're going to be grandma and grandpa." Selena laughed a hard, mirthless laugh. "But Barney don't know it yet," she whispered and looked fearfully toward the front of the store.

Maia stared uncomprehendingly across the cracked tabletop. The ceiling fan gently pushed warm air down on the two women, who sat motionless. The memory of Herman rising godlike from the water flashed through her mind. "That child! And your daughter…it can't be…he wouldn't…"

"That child, my foot! That 'child' has more smarts than you and me together, and more tricks, and more lies…" Selena's voice cracked.

"Why didn't you tell me? Why didn't you come to me? He's…well, he's not my responsibility, but I've let him use that shack, it gave him a way to stay here, around Canthy…"

Maia still couldn't accept the fact that, during Herman's absences, he had been dallying—lying with—the classic euphemisms came to mind. Maia was shocked at the fury and violence of her reaction. The boy she had grown to believe, to love as her own son…she could hardly breathe.

She looked up at the brown blades of the fan, turning lazily around. The moving air pushed a wisp of hair from her sweaty forehead. And then the image appeared again, Herman rising from the river in his aura of godlike beauty, his strong, slim body, the water sparkling on his shoulders. She put her hand to her mouth, eyes closed. She glanced at Selena, then shut her eyes again, unable to face Selena's curious stare.

She, Maia, was jealous! Jealous! What a mean, small word to define what had seemed the best and finest time of her life. It had turned to petty jealousy! Over a boy!

Chapter 11

MAIA HAD MET the rebellious Canthy a few times when spring lettuce and radishes from the Frang gardens were ready to make their flamboyant appearance at the general store. Canthy had brought them, brilliant and dew fresh, into the store through the back door and slammed the flat wooden boxes angrily on the counter as if to be rid of them once and for all.

Except that Canthy was almost as large as her mother, Maia would have called her a miniature of Selena. Canthy had Selena's fine pale hair, blowsy and tightly permed. Maia could imagine mother and daughter winding each other's hair on the tiny plastic rollers from the home permanent boxes on the general store's shelves, Selena happily, Canthy grudgingly.

Like Selena's, Canthy's face was a perfect full moon, punctuated by small, wary eyes and a freckled pug nose. The mouth was small, with a bow of full lips. But Canthy's gap teeth rarely showed in a smile like Selena's ready, sunny warmth. Instead, the mouth wore an almost continual pout every time Maia saw her. She moved in her oversized T-shirt like a billowing cloud, a storm ready to break forth. Maia had thought her cut-off jeans, pulled taut over bulging thighs, gave much the same impression. Canthy seemed to harbor a smoldering resentment against the world. Maia hadn't known how to approach her, and had not done so, except to murmur a greeting when Selena introduced them.

And now she was faced with the thought of the silent, angry, unresponsive Canthy with Herman…with exciting, vibrant, volatile Herman. Intimately with Herman. Maia's initial blinding rage slowly faded into a blend of dismay, disillusion, and an old familiar sense of abandonment. These had been the products of her confrontation with Tim. His warm smile had turned cold at the word "pregnant." These had been her bedfellows as she lay, trying to figure what to do, as she faced the grim reality of an expanding waist and diminishing options.

Well, her waist was not expanding now. Maia suddenly, irrationally, wished it were. This time she would keep her baby, she thought. This time she would have something left. She would not be alone.

But as she shook her head to chase away the outrageous thought, she became aware of Selena's face across the table. The usually firm round cheeks seemed to sag into folds beside the tiny mouth. The ruddy skin had turned pasty, and the eyes had lost their wary snap.

"Oh, Selena! Oh, my dear!" Maia was surprised at the sudden deep sympathy she felt for the haggard woman across the table, a woman she had thought of as merely an adjunct to the store, a convenience for her. Although giving up Peter those years ago was a far cry from Canthy's pregnancy, both in time and personal significance, Maia sensed the kinship of failed motherhood, the wrenching guilt that somehow a serious mistake in parenting could have—should have—been prevented.

As she reached across the table to grasp Selena's hand, footsteps sounded from down one of the cluttered aisles, and Phineas Solon appeared behind Selena. Maia hadn't seen him since Selena had introduced them a few weeks before. He exuded an insolent vitality, almost an aura of electricity. He was taller than Maia remembered. *But of course he was sitting when I saw him before,* she reminded herself. He wore a khaki-colored work shirt opened halfway to his belt, exposing a deep, black V of curly chest hair. His grimy jeans were cinched around a slim waist with a large, shell-buckled belt. His cap was pushed back on his head, the visor forming a gold-colored arch above a tousle of dark, shiny curls. His dark eyes under silky, straight, black brows were set narrowly beside a thin, aquiline nose. They darted and stabbed the dark corners of the grocery area, but stopped when he saw the women holding hands. His suggestive, knowing grin revealed perfect white teeth.

"Well," he drawled, "what have we here? A budding... friendship?" and he winked broadly at Maia. She withdrew her hand almost guiltily and lifted her chin defiantly. Selena shook her head at Maia in a barely visible warning. *Canthy's situation isn't widely known,* Maia thought, and then with another angry twinge wondered just when the coupling had taken place. *Some evening after Herman laughed with me and left my table? Maybe every evening?*

But she nodded civilly to Phineas, which he took as an invitation to join them. "How about a beer, Selena?" The rigid finger he poked at her soft side disappeared to the first knuckle. "You been loafing on the job long enough! And you, Miss Prescott?" he turned to Maia with exaggerated politeness. "That coffee looks cold—you won't get much of a kick out of it—you want a beer, too?"

Maia was prepared to refuse anything Phineas Solon offered, but as she glanced down at the cold black coffee, the brown lines left from each swallow circling the inside of the white plastic cup, its bitter taste filled her mouth, and she surprised herself by saying, slightly embarrassed, "Well, yes, a beer would taste good...but I'll pay for it myself."

Phineas leaned back in his chair and surveyed her with approval. "Whatever you wish, madam. I presume you want it in a glass?"

"Yes, please, Selena," Maia said softly, and felt herself redden.

Selena hoisted herself off the creaking, rusting metal chair and shuffled toward the cooler. Phineas continued to gaze at Maia with a slight smile. She pushed her cup back and glanced across the table at him. His eyes, dark and probing, held hers. Maia was shocked at their intensity. They seemed to delve deep into her very being: her present, her past, even her future. They seemed to discern everything about her. Unnerved, she forced herself to lower her own eyes to her cup. *This is ridiculous,* she thought. *He can't know me...I've only met him once. He is just an ordinary man—with an extraordinary presence. Is it this place or am I losing my grip on reality? Why do everything and everybody seem to have an extra bizarre dimension?*

Maia's thoughts were interrupted when Selena brought two sweating brown bottles and a clear glass, set them unceremoniously in front of Phineas, and collapsed again on the protesting chair. Maia groped in her purse for a tissue, wiped her forehead, and closed her eyes for a moment behind the tissue. It was so warm in the close, semi-lit grocery area. When she looked up again, Phineas was filling her glass.

He handed the glass filled with amber liquid to Maia. Tiny bubbles rose in it to join the foam at the top. Maia smiled her thanks at Phineas and took a deep drink. She hadn't tasted a beer for a long time, probably years. And its salty, acrid taste seemed unfamiliar. She took another swallow, breathed deeply, and looked up. "Mr. Solon..."

"Phineas—no, Phiny to my—friends," he said, and hitched his chair toward her. She withdrew imperceptibly.

"Well, Phineas—have you by any chance seen my dog, Kastor? He's a little gray dog, has long fur and kind of a mustache. He ran away last night—he's never done that before."

Phiny's black eyes again looked directly into Maia's. "No, haven't seen him—today." The eyes held hers another long moment before he tipped his brown bottle for a long draught.

"Well, have you seen him before today? Yesterday?"

"Yeah, I seen him sometimes when you two hiked down the road. Looked like a nice little dog."

"Do you think—are there any children he might have followed? Although he has never known any children," she added almost to herself.

"Well, there's the Proberson kids," Selena volunteered. "They ain't got much to do in summer—and not much to do with, neither. They mighta took the dog for a new plaything."

Maia looked from Selena to Phineas. *Why do I think he knows everything?* she asked herself angrily.

"S'pose they coulda," Phineas allowed after a long pause and another pull from the brown bottle. "Hope not, though. They're mean little sons o' bitches—Oh, beg your pardon, Miss Prescott," he added elaborately.

Alarmed, Maia leaned toward him. "Mean? You think they would hurt him?" The thought that anyone would harm Kastor, her one firm friend, sickened her.

"Dunno—never can tell what some kids'll do. But naw! I wouldn't worry 'bout it. Dog'll probably show up. He maybe just got the urge for some pretty little female. Happens, you know." He winked at Maia.

"No—no—he's been neutered—he has never…" She stopped at Phiny's obvious pleasure in her confusion. She took a long drink from her glass, draining it. She dug a few bills from her purse, told Selena to keep the change, and pushed her chair back. "I'll talk with you again soon."

"Hey, you ain't gettin' huffy, are you? We was just talkin' dogs, you know," Phiny chuckled.

"No, I'm not—huffy." Maia had to smile at the word. "I just should get back to Doria; maybe Kastor came home." *And I have so much to think about, and so much I don't even want to think about,* she added to herself. *And you, Mr. Phineas Solon, aren't going to make it all any easier.*

Chapter 12

MAIA STARED DOWN AT THE ROAD as she walked slowly along the route that earlier had been a source of such delight. The sun, risen to mid-morning strength, beat hard on her head and shoulders. The birds has quieted from their early exuberance. The day seemed to be holding its breath against the sawmill smell, which had edged out the aroma of flowers.

Maia turned to look back at The Place. It squatted in the same broken line. The shadows from the roof angles had changed as the sun rose, but still invited an attempt at a painting. Suddenly the vision of the car, spurting dust and stones as it pulled away from the general store, came to Maia's mind. That car...why did it seem so familiar? She knew so few people here, and surely didn't know what kinds of cars they drove—if they drove cars. The haze of dust had partially obscured the car as it drove away from her, but Maia knew she had seen it before. And then it came back: it was the same old dark blue sedan she had so eagerly awaited the day she first saw Doria. And it had pulled away from the house on Chestnut Street with the same spinning of wheels after she stepped into it. That had been Andy Turrick's car pulling away from The Place!

After her initial shock, Maia had almost to smile. Was Andy doing an appraisal on the General Store? But if he had business in the area, why didn't he come to see her? Then she recalled his last visit—his watching her from the bushes, his evasive answers about Doria, her angry stalk into the house, leaving him standing on the drive. She supposed he didn't feel very welcome. Well, he hadn't been very welcome just then. And he really had no reason to stop. He was just the leasing agent, and she had paid her rent on time. Still, Maia felt a stab of disappointment. He had been, after all, instrumental in her being at Doria. And although he had seemed not to want her here, he had made it possible. His name was on the lease with hers.

The heat of the asphalt road burned through the thin soles of her shoes. The hot sun and the effects of the rapidly drunk, unfamiliar beer made her head distinctly light. She forgot about Doria, about her mother, Peter, Herman. She even forgot about Kastor, whose immediate fate she ought to think about.

Instead she let her thoughts hover around Andy. She decided she couldn't call him handsome—handsome, for instance, as Phineas was handsome, with his regular classical features, tall, slender, and athletic looking. No, Andy was…well…just sturdy…rugged and rough hewn like a chunk of granite resisting smoothing by wind or weather or wild waves. His short, stocky build wouldn't win any Mr. America contests, she decided, but she figured he'd hold his own in a tussle. *Now why did I think of a fight?* she wondered. She didn't usually judge people by their combative capabilities! It was just that she thought, should the occasion demand it, that Andy would step in and stop a fight. Then Phineas slipped into the picture again. Phiny, on the other hand, would probably stand back, watch the blood flow, and bet on the winner!

She could clearly see Phiny in her mind, standing at ease, arms folded, watching a street fight with those black, cynical eyes, an anticipatory smile playing around the full lips. At that precise moment, she heard a footstep right behind her, and a muscular arm slipped easily around her waist. She jumped, gasped, and turned to see in reality the very face she had been thinking of—the same cynical eyes, the same anticipatory smile. Phiny fell into step beside her and looked down into her startled face.

"Having a pleasant walk, Miss Prescott? Sun's kind of warm, though, ain't it?"

Maia moved slightly away from Phiny but not out of the circle of his arm. "Uh...yes, it is hot...*warm!*" she corrected herself quickly.

Phiny grinned broadly down at her. "Oh, 'hot' is all right with me! In fact, I like 'hot,' Miss Prescott. Can I walk you home? Isn't that the way nice, 'warm,' old-fashioned relationships start? You are old fashioned...or are you?"

"Yes...no...I'm not old fashioned...I don't think..." Phiny seemed to enjoy her confusion. "I'm quite able to get home myself. See how close we are," she added firmly as they turned to walk up the drive.

"Oh, I know you can, but I thought you might get lonely today, without your dog. Nobody should be lonely on a nice day like this! Especially beautiful young women!"

Maia didn't answer, just moved along in step with Phiny's heavy brown shoes, her own sandal-clad feet looking small and vulnerable beside them. How long had it been since anyone had called her beautiful? And how good Phiny's arm felt!

Taking her silence for consent, Phiny tightened his arm again slightly and the pressure urged her a bit faster up the gravel drive, through the shadows of pines, up toward the tall, white pillars of Doria.

Chapter 13

A FEARFUL HEADACHE was her first impression as she lay with her eyes closed. She couldn't even remember where she was. Cautiously she spread her fingers along the rumpled sheets beside her. The faint rectangles of her unshaded windows were the first thing she saw when she finally opened her eyes. A slight breeze wisped the willow branches against the wall and rustled the tall pines. It seemed to be night.

Maia lay perfectly still, willing her head to stop throbbing in order to orient herself. Why was it night? She remembered hot sun…ice cold drinks…shadows playing on the patio…shadows touching Phiny's lips…sunlight touching Phiny's shining curls…her fingers curling into Phiny's crisp curls. And a sense of ecstatic exhilaration she had never experienced before. She closed her eyes again and let the memory wash over her in warm waves.

She could remember no more. She simply could remember nothing beyond that total pleasure...how day passed into night...how she came to be in her bed. Her head seemed to explode as she moved it to clear her mind. Suddenly she was in another bed, a bed in her mother's house. Again she was struggling to recall how she had gotten there, struggling to fill in the black void with something...something she didn't really want to remember—whatever it was that came after that horrifying moment with the pillow, her mother's eyes sunken in her emaciated face, eyes half open, unseeing, the warm closeness of the shaded room. She couldn't...didn't want to remember it.

Then somehow she had awakened in her bed with old Dr. Sampson talking quietly with Ida Riker, one of her mother's friends, over in the corner. It was night, then, too. When she had moved, started to push herself up. Dr. Sampson, with Ida right behind him, crying, had come close to tell her that her mother was dead. Maia had waited silently for him to accuse her, to hold up the pillow, covered in pastel brocade, to show where the final struggling, gasping breath had made indelible marks amid the pale pink flowers and green leaves of the fabric. Tell her that the police were on the way. Maia's heart beat hard and fast as it had that night, a fine mix of fear for the future and exhilaration over what was done. The doctor did not tell her that, however.

But there was no one here now, no caring Dr. Sampson or gentle Ida Riker to help her into the next act in this strange drama in which she seemed to be the only player. As she moved toward the edge of the bed, holding her hands to her head, she saw the shadow of the gray cat as it leaped silently from the window ledge into the brush outside. If only cats could talk, Maia thought, and if I could catch it, that cat could tell me many things.

Then she thought of Kastor, who should have been guarding her bed. And the painful memory of Kastor's running away struck home again, bringing her back to the beginning of reality. I've got to look for him...but not now...it's night. He's been gone a whole day and two nights...he must be hungry! Oh, Kassie!

She looked down at her wrinkled cotton skirt, at her thin white blouse that was twisted awry, the buttons straining. Her clothes, though rumpled, were intact. She had to face the fact that Phiny had put her in her bed, but he seemingly had done nothing else. Maia wondered, briefly and irrationally, why not.

As she swung her bare brown legs over the side of the bed and put her feet to the floor, her sandals were exactly where she could slip into them. She wondered, hopefully, for a moment, if she had indeed put herself to bed. Or was Phiny, under that rough, cynical, insinuating exterior, a sensitive, aware person who would think ahead to her waking comfort? She stood, and her head, with one last mighty, rebellious throb, settled down to a dull ache. Maia kept a hand on the wall as she eased herself from the bedroom into the shadowy living room and turned on the reading lamp. The room was empty. She glanced into the kitchen; it too seemed empty. Two green glasses stood on the cupboard, throwing tall shadows on the wall behind them. What had she drunk from them to make her lose hours of her life? Or had she simply experienced another blackout like the one last April?

Maia turned back to the bathroom and clung to the edge of the sink as she looked at herself in the mirror. Her thick hair was tousled and her mascara smudged. Her gray eyes stared wide, the pupils large and black. She splashed water on her face and rubbed it dry on a rough turkish towel, leaving the mascara in black smudges on the white nap. She combed her hair and smoothed it to a semblance of its usual simple page-boy. She brushed her teeth to clear the thick, sour taste from her mouth, found aspirin, and washed them down with a full glass of water.

By the time she settled with a cup of tea in the reading chair, the big square, curtainless living room windows were lightening. Random chirping sounded from the willows and pines. An occasional motor, muffled by the trees and thick underbrush, growled around the curve below the drive.

For the first time since she had arrived at Doria, Maia felt the claustrophobia which had driven her from her mother's house. She went to the front door and pulled the heavy oak-paneled door open. As she leaned against the door jamb, moths beat against the screen, trying to get to her reading lamp, trying to get to her. Maia could almost feel their powdery wings on her face, beating at her eyes, catching in her breath.

As she looked over the wide expanse of trees and gray sky turning pearly gray in the dawn, she began to feel the gentle calming that nature's beauty always brought her. Until her glance fell on the patio. There, tossed carelessly over the table, were the sheer green curtains from her mother's bedroom. A few days before, she had been hemming them after deciding to hang them over her own bedroom windows, partly to foil the gray cat. She had been working on them in the living room, under the lamp, hadn't she? Had she brought them outside?

She pushed at the screen door, disturbing the hovering moths, and walked slowly toward the curtains. They looked phosphorescent in the pale dawn, almost like folded moonbeams. As she lifted the curtains, one fell, as if weighted, from her hand. A large shell, of shining soft, sky colors, fell from the green folds.

Maia knew that shell! Phineas had worn it on his belt. She picked it up. It gathered and held two corners of a curtain together. As if in a trance, or as part of a ritual, or as if she had done it many times, Maia slowly slipped the diaphanous fabric over her head, the green folds falling softly to the patio stones, the shell firmly on one shoulder. She pushed her heavy hair up, twisted and held it in a knot at the top of her head. She turned to stare at her reflection in the living room windows. The slim columns framed the tall figure in flowing robes. The shell on her shoulder caught the first rays of the sun as it slipped over the trees on the eastern horizon. Maia put her other hand up to touch the shell.

Just then flute sounds wafted up from the copse of pines below…a sweet, unfamiliar melody, like a gift from the universe. For a seemingly endless moment, Maia knew who she was. She was the nymph, Maia, mother of Hermes, consort of Zeus and of uncounted Greek gods, member of a rare and enchanted company—Athena, Aphrodite, Dionysus, Ares, Apollo—at home on the Acropolis and Mount Olympus. She was home! It was a timeless moment of incomparable triumph.

But the sweet notes from below turned discordant and sour. The smooth rhythm became unruly and broken, a parody of the classical symphonia of a moment before.

The broken music shattered Maia's euphoria. She was forced to think about the maker of the discordant music: Herman/Peter/Hermes was down in the shack playing his little flute. Herman-Peter-Hermes with his crisp black curls, his dark knowing eyes.

And suddenly, standing in the dawning light of a gentle June day, Maia understood how Phiny had captivated her in the space of a few minutes—how she had felt she knew him even as he seemed to know her to the very depths of her being.

Herman had laid the groundwork for her…her what? Her seduction? Had she been seduced? Phiny was Herman, matured! The strong, overwhelming, irrational desire Maia had felt for Herman, the boy-man-god rising from the water, had been transferred, in the shadowy reaches of the general store, to the very earthy man, Phineas, the local builder of houses. And Maia knew, in that moment, that Herman was Phineas' son.

She was instantly angry, an anger overcome by the sense of loss, that Herman was surely not Peter, her son. On the heels of that brief fury came another, this one directed at Phiny. Why didn't he take care of his son? Why was that boy living the life of a wandering bum, a degenerate, at sixteen?

At that moment, a motor roared around the corner of the drive and up the hill, to pull with a screech of brakes onto the parking area. Maia turned slowly, trying to bring this strange noisy apparition into harmony with her dreamlike experience and confused musings.

"What in hell are you doing?" Andy Turrick demanded roughly as he slammed the door of the old blue Buick and sprinted toward the patio.

Maia stared at him and in the next moment became Maia, museum curator, sometime artist, renter of Doria—and furious. It was Andy Turrick again, intruding on her life, spoiling her most intimate and joyous moments. She loosed her hair, let her hand fell from the shell on her shoulder, and found her very human voice. "What…what in…what are *you* doing?" she demanded back.

Andy was by this time striding across the patio. He wore gray slacks and a lightweight tweed jacket. His white shirt was open at the top, contrasting sharply with his deeply tanned throat. His hair was the usual tangle of gray and red, and gray-green eyes flashed with anger or worry. Maia didn't care which.

He gripped both her shoulders and searched her face. "Are you all right? Are you alone? What are you doing up so early?" And after glancing down at her clothes, "And what in God's name, are you doing in that get-up?"

Maia glared back at him and tried to shrug his hands from her arms. "I'm quite all right, thank you. What do you mean, charging up here and waking the entire hillside with your yelling?"

Seeming satisfied that she was in no immediate danger, Andy let his hands fall to his sides and looked slightly embarrassed. In a voice that passed for subdued, he apologized.

"Excuse me. I'm sorry if I startled you. But there's been a little…excitement…down at The Place last night…and…well…I wasn't sure…Are you alone?" he repeated.

"Yes, I'm alone! Except for *you*," Maia's emphasis was no endearment. Then the sense of what he had said hit her. "What excitement? At The Place? What happened?"

"It's a long story, Maia. Can we sit?" He looked over at the patio chairs, seemingly suddenly tired and in need of a place to rest.

"Yes, of course." Maia gathered her green gown gracefully in one hand, as if used to the motion, walked to the table, and pulled out two chairs. Andy followed her, collapsed in one of the chairs, and looked up at her.

"What in hell are you wearing?" His voice had regained its aggressive tone.

Maia hesitated. She couldn't tell him she wore her mother's curtains. She couldn't tell him it was a chlamys, the Grecian version of the Roman toga. She couldn't tell him the shell on her shoulder held magic powers that transported her to another age, another life.

"What I wear is not your concern! But what happened at The Place? Is everyone all right?" Maia thought of Selena, of Canthy and the unborn child. And she thought of Phineas—and of course, Herman, for whom Maia had recently found a niche in this uncommon community.

Andy didn't answer right away. "I guess if you mean 'no physical harm,' everyone is all right."

She flared up again. "Would you—could you—please tell me what happened? I guess...I slept...rather heavily last night, and I didn't hear any commotion."

"Guess there wasn't much commotion, just a few people running around in the dark. We...there was a drug bust...a little banging on doors."

"A drug bust! What in God's name do you have to do with drugs? Or drug busts? Is playing policeman a sideline to real estate?"

Andy laughed shortly. "No, I guess the real estate business is something of a sideline to police work. It has been a rather successful cover, actually."

"You're an undercover drug agent?" Maia's head was reeling with this latest identity change.

"You got it."

"Aren't you afraid I'll…don't they call it 'blow your cover'?"

"No, I'm sure my secret is safe with you."

"Was the 'bust' a success? Did you arrest anyone?" Maia tried to think of the few people she had seen at The Place, and whether any of them fit her concept of a drug dealer.

"Yes, we did arrest Barney Frang."

Maia gripped the arm of her chair. "Barney?" The inscrutable Barney had, in the last twenty-four hours, almost become family! He would be grandfather to Herman's child!

"Yeah, but we still have a few loose ends to tie up. There's Phineas Solon." Andy eyed her sharply. "Selena said…was he up here last night?" Maia just stared at him, her teeth clenched. "And Herman, your young friend down in the shack…"

"Herman! He's just a boy! You surely don't mean he's mixed up in this business?" Her sharp-voiced concern for Herman was an unconscious buffer for her other concern, which she couldn't speak now to Andy, which she would have to face…Phiny…drugs…that incomparable exhilaration she had known…the loss of several hours…drugs?

Her headache returned with a vengeance.

Chapter 14

ANDY GAVE MAIA NO TIME to pamper her headache. "That *boy* is quite an operator, Maia! We're pretty sure that *boy* has been running the stuff for over a year, packing it in his backpack, stashing it in the shack down the hill."

"What do you mean, 'running the stuff'? He doesn't even have a car!"

"He didn't need one. He hitched rides, seemed to charm drivers into picking him up. We've had an eye on him, just wanted to nail the big time, the one making the money."

Maia flared up defensively. "You mean Barney…you mean Barney has been selling…making money…on…drugs in this little backwater? This isn't even a town! Nobody here has any money…hardly enough for groceries. Didn't you see how Selena works to keep that store going? Making soup and bread, growing vegetables…I hate to tell you, drug agent Turrick, but I think you've made a big mistake! These people are scrambling to make a living!"

"That's their cover, honey…Maia," he corrected himself quickly as Maia flushed angrily.

"You mean Selena is in this thing too?" Maia still had in her mind the miserable mother who had sat at the table in The Place, feeling a failure because of her daughter's misadventures.

"Selena is in it up to her chubby chin," Andy said firmly. "Selena grew and sold a lot of marijuana along with her veggies."

"Did you arrest her?"

"Not yet. We'll wrap that up this morning…along with Solon and Herman. I wanted to warn you so in case there is resistance, you'll know what's going on."

"He…Herman was just playing his flute when you came charging up the hill…" Maia was still trying to put together all this new information, trying to fit it into her relationship with these people who so recently had become significant in her life—almost friends, about the only ones she had. "Does he…know…about the arrests?"

"Don't think so, or he'd have run. He's been on a short 'trip,' just got back early this morning, probably has a good supply of coke hanging on a nail in the shack right now."

Maia's mind was flooded with all her memories and dreams about Herman—that he was a boy who needed her; whom she had thought she could help; that he was very like…might even be…her son, Peter; that he had been transformed into the trickster/traveler/god Hermes as he emerged from the water and had wakened a kind of desire she had almost forgotten; and that he had suddenly become very ungodlike to her in his role as father of Canthy's child. And now he was involved…in drugs! Her throat all but closed in an overwhelming rush of maternal concern. He was still the thin, hungry boy who had wolfed down bread and cheese and olives at her table. "Can I see him…before…?"

"Well, I guess so." Andy studied her face. "Does he mean so much to you?" he asked gently.

"Yes…we are…were…friends. He's so young; so bright…could be so sweet…" her voice trailed off into silence as she gripped her hands together in her lap.

"Since he's there in the shack, this is as good a time as any. Then we can pick him up and get this business over this morning. But, listen, Maia. Don't go all soft over that kid. He's tough and hard as nails behind those big brown eyes."

"What do you mean? How do you know?"

"We've talked with some of the generous people unfortunate enough to have given him rides when he was hitchhiking. They didn't know what he was packing on his back. He soft-soaped them to make them feel at ease, then roughed them up and robbed them. Their testimony will help nail down this case. Herman…he's a con man by nature, Maia."

She sat quietly, folding and re-folding the green fabric on her lap. After a long silence… "And…did you say… Phineas…Solon?" She stared at the pleats her fingers held on her knees, as if it were important to keep them firmly in place.

Andy watched her in silence, the tousled hair, so recently held in a Grecian knot, bent low over the trembling brown fingers. "Yes," he said finally. "Phineas Solon. He's the local king in this sordid little business—and he's slippery."

"If you're so sure…if Selena said…why didn't you come up here last night? Why didn't you look for him here?"

"I didn't want to involve you," Andy said softly as her leaned toward her. "I didn't know…how things could go… you could have been hurt."

"If you knew he was here, why didn't you watch for him to come down?" Maia struggled with her conflicting loyalties…the apprehension of drug runners against her still vivid awareness of the electric presence of Phineas Solon. She couldn't resolve the two concepts. Not yet. Even as she faced Andy, his cool, gray eyes reflecting concern for her, she saw Phiny's smoldering eyes instead.

Andy's voice broke into her distraction. "We did watch. He got by. I said he was slippery."

"Do you know where he is now?"

"Not exactly." Andy's voice hardened. "Do you? The question rapped out like a hammer on steel.

"No. No, I don't know where he is." Maia wanted to admit that she didn't know anything for sure anymore. That reality seemed hopelessly mixed up with dreams. That she didn't even know who she was, or where her home was, here in Maine or on Mount Olympus. She wanted desperately to lay her confusion on those broad, tweed-covered shoulders across the table and not think about anything. She wanted to put her head down against that crisp white shirt and just go into a profound sleep.

But she knew she couldn't do that. She must see Herman, for the first time since his swim in the river, since he had emerged, golden, sun-sparkled, otherworldly in his aura of clean, bright beauty. Clean? Maia's stomach turned sickeningly as she remembered Andy's words: hard as nails. Con man by nature.

By nature. Hermes, by his very nature, was the "bad boy" of prehistory. On the very day he was born in a cave, he stole Apollo's cattle, drove them backward to confuse his pursuers, then, when caught, claimed he was too young for such a nefarious crime. He made his lyre from a tortoise shell and, carrying his snake-wound caduceus, wandered the world, playing tricks on the gods. He was their messenger, but he was also the patron of thieves, gamblers, orators, and commerce. Did his contemporaries blame him for his shifty nature? Or was Hermes accepted simply as a side of nature with which the world in which he existed would live? Could this present world of law tolerate a Herman, a twentieth-century "bad boy"?

Would this world excuse with a smile and a wink Herman's "natural" inclination to deception, manipulation, and disdain for the law?

Of course not. His considerable charm would not deflect the legal results of his actions, Maia knew. But she had to see him once more before those results hit him. She was afraid. Afraid for him, afraid of him. Afraid of and for herself. But she knew she must see him.

She stirred in the white-painted chair. The carefully pressed pleats in the pale green chlamys fell apart. "All right. I'll go down now. Will you be here?"

"I'm going to run down to The Place. Barney has been taken to Pembroke, but we'll pick up Selena when she comes to the store. She may know something about Solon. Maybe she'll talk. Barney clammed up. Listen, Maia. You have your little time with Herman. But don't tip him off. You know how important this is, don't you? This damn drug thing is a losing battle, but we have to win every skirmish we can. Just…well… just be natural, be nice to him, say whatever seems right, but don't let him know we've broken this set-up. He's a juvenile, so the courts will go easy. But it'd be no favor to let him go on the way he is." Andy paused, looking intently at Maia, who was still staring at her hands. "Maia, are you hearing me?"

"Yes, yes, I hear you. Don't tip him off. Be natural. Yes." She stood, and the green fabric, in the glare of the strengthening sun, had become simply a pair of sheer curtains, haphazardly draped on Maia's shoulders. Embarrassed, she pulled them over her head. They fell to the patio, the shell fastener breaking on the stone.

Andy rose tiredly, put his hand briefly on Maia's arm, and walked quickly across the patio to his car. Maia heard the motor start, heard the gravel crunch under the tires as Andy turned the wheels sharply and drove down the driveway.

She straightened her blouse, smoothed her skirt, then her hair, and started slowly down toward the shack through the rough weeds, by now hip high. They scratched her legs and pulled at her sandals. Insects and dust flew up, but Maia was oblivious to them. What would she say to Herman? Would she be able to hold this short time within the emotional boundaries she most wanted and needed to remember… those happy times when Herman was a needy boy and she was his friend? Did she dare mention Canthy's—and his—baby? Could she control her inclination to tell him to run—run as fast as he could? To survive in freedom in any way he could?

She remembered his flashing anger whenever she had pushed too close to those invisible defenses he had built around himself. If he flared at her, a caring and nonthreatening person, how would he handle the restraints of the justice system? He would break. She knew it. He would do something violent and make his case worse. She envisioned him snaring himself deeper and deeper into the horrors of the penal world where he would surely perish.

Maia rounded the corner of the shack. On the ground, the brown twisted strands of last May were gone, buried under fresh new tangles of green. Next year, the green, in turn, would be brown and dead.

There was no sound except Maia's footsteps and the drone of insects. She realized the flute music had long been silent. The door of the shack was ajar. She knocked gently on it, and it swung silently open. The shack was empty. The vine-twisted walking stick, the shell-covered guitar, the bedroll and blanket. Herman. All gone. The silence hung like dusty drapes in the small dark room. Maia looked for the knapsack Andy said would be hanging on a nail. Gone.

She took a deep breath in the musty air. Her throat hurt. She would not see him again. But he was gone, free, and she had not warned him. She had not had to make that fearful decision. Something in the complicated personality that was Herman had warned him. Maia thought back to the flute music at dawn. Perhaps that magic moment which had transformed her into a goddess had made him Hermes and given him godlike powers of perception, assuring that he would continue free as Hermes, the traveler.

Tears welled up as Maia recalled that first meeting. She had stood where she stood now when Herman had identified himself...as a traveler. And she heard him ask, "Ever see a boy who wasn't hungry?"

"Herman/Hermes/Peter...may your travels be safe," she murmured aloud.

The sound of her own voice brought her back to the present. Andy. Andy would be furious. Would he believe she had not warned Herman? Maia decided that would have to be Andy's problem, not hers. She looked around once more at the bare, rotting floor, the dusty windows curtained with cobwebs, the haphazard shelves. A dull, white reflection in the clutter of dusty bottles and slouching paper bags on the shelf caught her eye. She moved across the squeaking floor, dust puffing up at each step, and picked it up. It was a small pipe, like a child's flute. It seemed to be made of bone or ivory. Was this the instrument on which Herman made his music—the magic music that had transformed her a little while before?

She imagined it was still warm from Herman's hands. Why had he left it, when he had left nothing else—no good-bye, no thanks, no hope for a future meeting?

Maia slipped the little flute into her skirt pocket, walked slowly to the door, and looked back once more. As she pulled the door shut after herself, she knew she would not come here again.

Chapter 15

She paused on the flat stone step, breathed deeply, and looked around at the small clearing. This had been Herman's backyard, where he had probably stretched out in the evening on the flattened grass, where he had played his shell-faced guitar, probably where he had drunk that foul-smelling wine, where the feral cats had doubtless clung about his ankles, crept onto his lap. Had the gray cat somehow told him, from its vigils on her window ledges, what she ate, where she sat, how she slept?

There were a couple of slight breaks in the wall of brush on the rim of the clearing. She edged her way onto a path which seemed to lead in the direction from which she thought she'd heard Kastor bark—how long ago? She didn't know what she hoped to find, but pushed ahead anyway. After the events of the past hours, her devotion to Kassie was the only thing of which she was sure.

The morning sun was almost completely blotted out by the dense leafage above, showing only as bright pinpoints like stars in a black night. As the path twisted and the stiff, scratching brush closed in behind her, Maia felt she had entered a strange twilight world where she traveled alone to some unknown destination. She called out hopelessly for Kassie a few times in a soft, tentative voice. But only a slight rustle of the leaves above answered.

Just as she broke through a particularly dense and forbidding clump of bushes onto a small clearing, her foot caught on what she thought was a fallen log. But her eyes widened in horror when she saw Kastor's bloated body on the edge of the grass. A fetid odor rose from it, along with a swarm of insects. Maia screamed, and her early morning tea rose in her throat. After the nausea passed, she leaned close again. She wanted to hold him, to bring him back by the sheer strength of her need for him. She had time only to see a cord wrapped tightly around his neck before the stench forced her back again.

"Don't think you can do much for him," Phineas Solon appeared out of nowhere, and that sure, strong, strangely familiar arm pulled her away from the dog's body and into the clearing. Maia looked up at him, unable to speak. "I came back to bury him," Phineas continued in the face of her silence.

"Phiny! Oh, Phiny! He's dead! My Kassie is…horribly dead! How…how did you know he was here? I thought…"

"It's a long sordid story, my dear, one you don't need to hear." He guided her to a large, flat-topped rock around which the grass had been almost worn away. Before he lifted her onto it, he reached into a crevice of the rock, retrieved two small plastic bags containing a white substance, and stuffed them into his pocket. Then he leaned toward her, a hand on each side of her hips. His face came close to hers. Maia caught her breath again as she experienced the deep, knowing look of those dark eyes. She felt she would almost drown in them.

With great effort she spoke. "But Kassie…you said… was it yesterday? You said you hadn't seen him. How did you know he was here…and…*dead?*

"Well, I knew he was dead because I killed him," he said matter-of-factly. Maia stared at him. "It was…necessary… Kassie came ripping in here, started barking, interrupting a very important meeting—a very important *private* meeting."

"You! You killed Kassie?" Phineas, of the caressing hands, Phineas of the gentle eyes. Maia recoiled from the face within inches of her own, and pushed at the strong hands at her sides. "Kassie wouldn't hurt you! He wouldn't hurt anyone! Why would anyone…*kill* him? He's been strangled. I saw the cord. Did *you* do that? Why?"

"I strangled him because it was the quietest way. I told you he burst in here barking…we couldn't have any noise. Might bring in unwelcome visitors."

"What were you doing here? This is Doria property, isn't it? I think Andy said it reached over to the road..."

"Andy? Who's Andy?" Phineas asked sharply as he backed away for a moment.

The almost unbelievable story Andy had told her about his real work and the residents of The Place flooded back into her mind. How should she answer Phiny? What could she say that would not jeopardize Andy's work, or even endanger him? She was sure anyone who could kill Kastor could and would do almost anything. "He...he's the...the real estate agent who helped me rent Doria..."

Phineas stared at her for what seemed endless time, his eyes probing deep, deep into her mind. Maia wondered fearfully if they could see Andy's secret work. "Has he been around here lately?" His dark eyes narrowed and he looked suddenly threatening as he leaned close again to Maia. She backed away, losing her balance, and almost fell on her back atop the huge, level rock.

"No! No! Why would he be back here?"

"Never mind." Phineas moved abruptly away. "I gotta go. But first I'll take care of the dog." He picked up the spade he had dropped when he had lifted her onto the rock. Maia lowered her eyes past the black chest hair. The shell buckle on Phineas' belt had been replaced with one of heavy brass. She watched as he removed the sod near Kastor's body and carefully put it aside. But she looked away when he began digging. She stayed seated on the rock and stared unseeing into the trees as the harsh sounds of the spade grating against the small stones of the earth filled the clearing. Now she knew. Kassie was dead. He wouldn't ever push up on his hind legs at the foot of the bed, cock an ear, and peer over her knees to see if she was awake. They would never again race down the Doria driveway and around the curve to The Place. He would never sit patiently, even if his leash slipped from the unpainted bench, waiting for Maia to come out of the general store. She would never feel that wiry gray hair and look into those trusting eyes. She forced herself to look at Phineas, methodically piling spades full of black earth onto the grass.

"If you could kill him, if you could be that cruel…why would you care about burying him? He's dead! He can't feel anything! He won't know if he's buried…or left to…" Her anguish circled the clearing like a trapped animal.

"I'm not doing it for Kassie, baby—I'm doing it for me. A strangled dog lying about might cause questions. And I was coming up here anyway. And I'm doing it for you, sort of thanks for the good time we had yesterday. Remember?" He had pushed the dog into the hole and was replacing the dirt and sod. He looked up when Maia didn't answer. "Remember?" he asked again as he caught and held her eyes.

"Remember? Of course! You walked me home…up the drive…we…had a cold drink…" her voice trailed off. She was probing her memory for what came next.

Phineas jabbed the spade into the newly replaced sod. It stood upright, a marker for the dead body below it. He rubbed his hands on the sides of his pants and walked back to the rock. His teeth shone brilliant white in the dark tan of his face. "That's right—a cool drink. Nice place, the Doria patio. I never got invited there before. We had a good time, didn't we?"

"I…I don't…quite remember."

Phiny smiled again at her blush.

"I bet you remember some of it. And I bet we could have a good time again. I bet this nice big rock is just as nice a place as that Doria patio. Whadaya think?" He was leaning toward her again, his arms a vise at her sides, his eyes riveting her immobile. The air was thick with tension. A sudden breeze moved the branches high above them in a conspiratory whisper, moved down and along the ground in a loud rustle, then stopped abruptly as the bushes parted and Andy stepped into the clearing, a short black gun in his hand.

Phineas stiffened when he saw Maia's eyes pull away from his and focus behind him. Without turning, he yanked her from the stone and, with one movement, forced her in front of himself as he turned.

Andy stopped, his face losing momentarily its stony sureness. "Maia! You said you didn't know…!"

"I didn't! Andy, I didn't know! Oh!" she grimaced in pain as Phineas twisted her left arm high behind her back. "Phiny! Don't! You're hurting me!"

"Shut up! Or you might get hurt a lot more!"

After a pause, he said sarcastically, "And so this is Andy, the real estate agent." He twisted her arm higher. "Are you some kind of 'agent' too, Maia? Acting so sweet and innocent?"

Andy started to move toward them, then stopped as Maia screamed in pain. Phineas twisted her arm ever higher, and clamped his other hand over her throat. She could hardly breathe. His hand tightened as she tried to twist free.

"We are going to move out of here, Maia and me, down that path," Phineas said with an iron edge to his voice. He nodded toward the path from which Andy had emerged. "And you, real estate agent Andy, are not going to stop us. I can break this pretty neck with one good yank—real fast—so keep your distance!"

Phineas began backing around Andy, dragging Maia with him. As she stumbled backward, the grip on her arm was even more painful. It felt as if her shoulder was pulled from its socket. Andy turned to watch their retreat, the gun useless in his hand.

Just as they moved into the brush at the edge of the clearing, Phineas' knees suddenly buckled and he fell backward, pulling Maia with him. His hands relaxed their grip as he fought to catch his balance. As Maia wrenched free, she fell sideways, and was shocked to find herself on the ground beside Selena Frang, who had wrapped her substantial arms firmly around Phineas' knees.

The next moments were filled with screams, curses, scuffles, snaps of breaking branches, and crunch of undergrowth trampled underfoot as Andy joined the group scrambling for footholds among the trees. Maia freed herself from the tangle as Andy pounced on a violently struggling, off-balance Phineas. Phineas desperately grabbed for Andy's gun, but only spun it off into the brush. Maia retrieved it and watched helplessly as the men struggled. She thought briefly of her earlier comparison of the two men—how each of them would handle confrontation. This time, Phineas had no chance to stand back and take bets on the winner. He himself would be either winner or loser. And this time, Andy was not trying to stop a fight; he had to win it, for his own and for Maia's sake and safety.

The two seemed evenly matched: Andy's training against Phineas' animal instincts and workman strengths. The deciding factor was Selena, who, down on the ground, stayed clear of most of the blows, and was able to keep Phineas off balance by gripping his legs.

After what seemed like a long time, but was probably only seconds, Andy was able to pinion Phineas' arms behind him and clamp handcuffs on his wrists. Except for the sound of the heavy breathing of the antagonists, the woods returned to relative silence. Phineas, backed against a tree, stared at Maia, but the magic of the dark eyes was gone. She no longer felt the strength, the will-draining fascination which had held her very being in their gaze. Those eyes now simply held hatred. Maia shivered and fervently hoped she never looked into them again when Phineas was free.

Selena pushed her massive body up from the forest path and brushed the leaves from her cotton dress. She looked at Maia, too. Maia, the gun still held awkwardly in one hand, moved over toward Selena and hugged her. She didn't think of Andy's accusation about Selena's marijuana garden. She didn't even take time to wonder that Selena was out in the woods with Andy, and could think only that she had saved Maia from Phineas. Later she would wonder why Selena had been so obviously proud to introduce her to this Phineas, who could turn on her so violently.

Only then did she turn to Andy who stood, still panting from exertion, watching the silent drama under the trees. Maia stepped over to him, handed him the gun which felt strange in her hand, and looked seriously up at him. She felt a strong twinge of her usual anger at him, that he kept interfering in her life, and somehow he had gotten her into this whole mess. But that brief fury was overwhelmed with a rush of gratitude that he had also gotten her out of it. "Andy...oh, Andy, thank you! Thank you for coming..." and she lay her forehead against that crisp white shirt.

Chapter 16

AN UNEASY SILENCE hung over the four as they waited in the general store for a government car to come for Phineas. He sat sullenly on a chair apart, refusing to say anything until he talked with a lawyer. Andy sat near him, watching him intently.

Selena, after her initial flush of pleasure at how she had prevented Phineas from harming Maia, seemed to be having second thoughts about her situation. She brought them each a cold drink from the cooler, then sat as quietly as the creaky metal chair would allow.

Maia had so many questions she didn't know where to start. She wanted to go back to the moment she had last sat on this very chair, holding Selena's hand in sympathy for

Selena's worries about her daughter. She wanted to continue that conversation about Herman and Canthy's baby, perhaps help Selena find a bright spot in the rather sordid picture they were painting for themselves. But would she have wanted to continue that conversation at the cost of Phineas' entrance? Maia knew it would take a very long time to sort our her feelings about that strange day and night, but she wasn't sure right now that she wished Phiny had not walked in at that moment, the golden yellow arch of cap atop the crisp black curls, the eyes crinkled with playful wickedness, the thumbs hitched in his belt next to the shell buckle.

Maia looked cautiously over toward him, his eyes downcast, his hands manacled uncomfortably behind his back. He seemed to feel her look, and glanced up, the anger still a live thing in his eyes.

Just then the front door of the store slammed and footsteps sounded down the long aisle. Two men in suits and ties came around the bread racks. Andy stood, greeted them, and led them over to where Phiny sat. He handed one of the men the plastic sacks he had taken from Phiny's pocket, told them to take him to Pembroke, and book him on attempted kidnapping, assault, and possession of unlawful substances. "And we'll figure the rest of the charges later," he growled as he hoisted Phiny off the chair.

Maia stared after the men as their footsteps receded into the dusky recesses of the general store. Now she could talk, now that Phineas' eyes couldn't intimidate her.

"Andy...how did you know how to find me? I was almost lost up there myself, the woods are so heavy and tangled..."

"Well, we have Selena to thank for that. Although she was a little reluctant to talk at first. And she didn't know she was taking me to you. I was looking for Phiny. You just happened," he added pointedly. "Anyway, a little reminder of Selena's high-priced garden produce helped her understand that she could help herself by cooperating. Right, Selena?"

Selena smiled faintly, the bow-lips straightening over the gap teeth, and nodded without speaking.

"Well, how did you know where I was, Selena?" Maia pressed her.

"I knew where...I knew the place...where they did their business...up there in the woods..."

"Business? What business?"

"You know. Drugs...coke...paying, dividing it, there on that big rock..."

Maia tried to picture midnight—or noon, for that matter—meetings of Phiny, Barney...Herman? Who else? All huddled around the flat stone where she had so recently sat, pinned down by Phiny's strong brown hands.

"But...why...did Phiny go there this morning? How did you know he went there today?"

Selena hesitated. "Well, it was...I think he figured Barney had left something up there. And then he was going to bury the dog...he didn't want you to find the dog, Maia...I think he was a little soft on you, Maia...and then he was going to get out. He knew Barney got picked up." Selena looked stricken, as if that fact had just struck her. "And he didn't want to get caught himself."

"I did find the dog, though!" and Maia's nausea began to return as she felt again Kastor's swollen body against her barefoot sandal. She swallowed hard and continued. "But you knew about Kassie when we sat here and talked…just the other day? Or was it yesterday?" Maia was still confused about the time elapsed since she and Kassie went down to the river to repair the picnic table. What a simple, everyday plan to turn into such a bizarre series of events! Maia ached for that kind of normalcy.

Selena was slow to answer. "Yeah…yeah, I knew your dog was dead. Phiny told me, but I couldn't tell you. Phiny woulda killed me!"

After a pause, she said, "Anyways, after a dog's dead, there's not much to do about it."

Maia had to agree with that hard fact, but she moved on. "Andy told me…about your…garden…about the marijuana…how could you get into such a business?" she asked in a voice that fairly cracked with indignation. Maia thought of Canthy and Herman. Were they users of Selena's products? And her heart stopped. The baby! Drug use could hurt Canthy's baby! "Does Canthy use…smoke…marijuana?" Her voice remained sharp with concern.

"No, not that I know. I warned her how dumb it was to start that stuff." After a pause, "Course, I warned her about Herman too, and that didn't do much good."

In answer to Andy's questioning look, Maia explained. "Andy, Selena's daughter is pregnant…it's Herman's baby…" and to Selena, in a fresh concern, "Oh, what will she do…now?" She in turn looked questioningly at Andy. "What will happen to Barney, and Selena?"

Andy shrugged. "Barney stands to do some time, I'd guess. But maybe we can plea Selena down to probation because she helped me find Phineas. He was the one we were really after."

"Selena, Phineas had been a friend and…business partner…for a long time. How could you turn on him?"

"Well, Andy…uh…Mr. Turrick here…persuaded me to at least show him where I thought Phiny had went…and I admit I felt bad about causing Phiny trouble. He's Herman's dad, you know, and it's looking like we'll all be related, with that baby coming and all…I kinda stayed in the woods so Phiny wouldn't see me and know I led Andy…Mr. Turrick…to him. But when it looked like he was going to hurt you, Mai…Maia…funny name! I just couldn't let him do it. So I had to tackle him myself."

Andy smiled. "That tackle just might keep you out of jail, Selena! But I am going to have to book you. We'll try to get a low bail so you can be out to be with Canthy. Why don't you lock up here and we'll go on into town? Hopefully we can bring you back this afternoon."

After Selena locked the front door of the general store, they all got into Andy's car. As he pulled away with his usual roar and spinning wheels, Maia looked back at the irregular doors, the cracked windows, the unpainted bench, and patched roofs of The Place. Then it all disappeared in a cloud of dust.

Chapter 17

For THE FIRST TIME since her mother's early rebukes, Maia was beginning to talk freely, of herself, of her pleasures in music and art, of her delight in the natural beauty of the world, even of her tangled relationships with her parents. On long walks along the hilly lanes and during leisurely meals and long warm evenings with Andy on the Doria patio, she slowly learned to share her innermost thoughts and concerns, which had been caged, circling, and going nowhere, in her head for years.

After the immediate excitement of the drug arrests settled down, Andy had gently asked Maia about Herman. Why wasn't he in the shack shortly after she visited him? Maia was able to tell him, in great relief, that she wasn't responsible, that he was gone when she got there, that she knew nothing more about where he was now. She even admitted she was glad he was gone, because she knew he would never survive imprisonment.

"But he was gone when I walked down to the shack." Andy seemed to believe her. "But will you…try to track him down?"

Andy's lips thinned. "He will, of course, be on the wanted lists. We have too much incriminating information to just let him go free." Then he paused at Maia's concerned face. "But he's…slippery…like his father. He could melt into the youth groups of any community and be pretty hard to find…not that we won't try!" he added quickly.

Maia tried to explain how her relationship with Herman had grown, how she was touched by his rootless existence, by his continuous ravenous hunger, how she had laughed at his humor and overlooked his mercurial changes of disposition and the mysteries of his erratic absences. But since Andy didn't yet know of Peter's existence, she didn't tell him how Herman had begun to be Peter. When Andy gently probed about Phiny, Maia was also restrained. She couldn't explain to herself, let alone to anyone else, even Andy—especially Andy—just what that relationship had been. It was already beginning to fade. Had it been with a real person or a figment of her imagination? Had she actually spent many hours with him? Had it been a sexual experience? Or had she been the victim of a strange dream? Or of a drug from one of Phiny's plastic packages? Or both?

"Phiny was…a man I met at the general store. Selena introduced us. He's a house builder, I believe."

Andy didn't press her for more details about him, but he did want to know how she happened to be with him in the clearing. He finally seemed to believe that she was at the flat rock with Phiny only as a result of looking—hoping—to find Kassie.

"But Kassie had been gone a couple of days already, Maia! Surely you didn't think he'd still be where you last heard him bark!"

"I don't know what I thought! Maybe I wasn't thinking!" she retorted a bit sharply. "I just knew I had to try something—anything—to find him…and I did find him," she added sadly.

As they spent more time together, hiking, attempting to bring some kind of order to the overgrown gardens, trying new recipes, repairing the picnic table by the river, Maia began to believe she could share with Andy the secrets which had brought her to Doria in the first place.

One evening as a light chill promised the advent of autumn, they built their first fire in the black fireplace. Andy insisted Maia sit in her one soft easy chair, while he sprawled on cushions at her feet. Maia finally felt comfortable enough to tell him, first of her baby, of her continuing sorrow over the adoption of Peter, then of her mother's death, and her part in it.

Andy was still a long time after she finished. Maia was afraid of what he was thinking. Then, "How have you been able to carry these...burdens...all alone? I think so much guilt, pushed down, denied, would drive you crazy!"

"Maybe it has! Maybe it has. Maybe I really am crazy," she repeated, silently recalling her experiences with Herman and Phineas.

"No, no! It hasn't. You aren't crazy...far from it! But you must resolve all this conflict or you might go over the edge yet!" He smiled up at her to lighten his words.

"Resolve them! How can I resolve them? They are done, the deeds are done. Peter is gone, I don't know where, and I've lost all those years with him. I will never know...how he is, how he looks, if he is happy. And Mother...she's gone, too, to a better world than she left, I hope. But I can't resolve my guilt over her death. Maybe I killed her! If I did, it was murder!" Hot tears streamed down her cheeks. She brushed at them with the back of her hand.

Andy rose, pulled her from her chair down to the cushion beside him. He wiped her tears and held her as she continued to sob. The relief of the tears was so great it hurt her entire chest. She thought it would explode.

When her sobs subsided to only an occasional hiccup, Andy gently suggested there might be ways to relieve her grief. "We'll get some facts. You've been chasing all kinds of horrible possibilities through your head for all these years—months, in your mother's case. Because you don't know, you imagine the worst. Tomorrow, we will go to the county courthouse and try to learn about Peter's adoption. They may not say where he is, but they can find out and tell you how he is, along with many details so you will rest easy. Then when we get that old trail warmed up, we will go to see Dr. Sampson. You have been living and re-living those few minutes in your mother's bedroom, but you are seeing them through the emotional haze of a distraught daughter. Dr. Sampson can give you the facts of your mother's death. Does that all make sense?"

Andy looked down at Maia. The hiccups had stopped. Her eyes were closed and she looked like a child ready for sleep. But when he stopped talking, her eyes opened and she looked up him. "That makes sense for tomorrow," she said slowly. "But for tonight, I'm so tired!"

As Andy helped her to her feet and they moved toward the bedroom, Maia reached up, ran her fingers through his short, wiry hair, and murmured softly, "Just like Kassie's!"

Chapter 18

THE SESSION IN THE RECORD DEPARTMENT of the county courthouse was a disappointment for Maia. She was primed to learn answers to questions about Peter she'd been pondering for sixteen years. But the person in the records office seemed reluctant to discuss even the fact that an adoption had taken place. The woman, Almira Kittridge, her hair pulled so tightly back it seemed to hold her eyes open, the sleeves of her white blouse so tight her chubby arms bulged below the edges, stared at her a long time after Maia stated her request. She had asked to be given any information legally available about her child, given up for adoption in February sixteen years before.

Miss Kittridge asked Maia for several kinds of identification, took them, and disappeared for many minutes into an inner office. Maia looked miserably over to Andy. It had been like ripping open a partially healed wound to state the details of Peter's birth to the icily staring Miss Kittridge. He squeezed her hand and smiled understandingly. "I know it hurts. It's the only way."

Miss Kittridge finally returned and coldly acknowledged that such a birth and subsequent adoption were indeed recorded. "But this is privileged information," she added firmly. "It is advised that you be given any details at all of such an adoption only after you have had counseling from a qualified social worker. In any case, you will not be told who his parents are, or where he is." Her stress on the word "parents" made Maia cringe. She was his parent! "People don't always like what they hear," she added in a somewhat menacing voice.

"What do you mean? Is Peter...not happy? Is he all right? Tell me!" Maia stood and leaned over Miss Kittridge's supremely orderly desk.

"No, Miss Prescott, I didn't mean anything of the kind. Please be seated, Miss Prescott!" She waited until Maia sat down again on the edge of her chair. "I only meant that sometimes people have developed unreal expectations about the happiness of children they have given up for adoption—possibly to soothe their own guilt feelings," she added almost under her breath.

"I don't have any preconceptions about Peter's situation," Maia objected. "How could I? I have no clues—all I know is his name."

"And that very likely has been changed," Miss Kittridge noted with a certain satisfaction.

Andy had sat quietly during this exchange. But he stood now. "Miss Kittridge, I believe Judge Anson Margerson makes final decisions regarding family court matters. How do I make an appointment with him?"

Miss Kittridge blinked, tossed her head, and glared up at him. "His office hours are from three to five P.M."

"Will you please make an appointment with him, preferably yet today?" Maia wasn't sure she could go through the necessary details again.

When they were ushered into Judge Margerson's paneled office, she took a deep breath and prepared to repeat them. But Andy moved ahead of her, clasped the gray-haired judge's hand, and was warmly greeted by him.

"Andy Turrick! Good to see you out of court!" He turned to Maia. "I see a lot of this fellow when young folks get themselves mixed up in the drug racket."

Andy smiled. "Judge, this is Maia Prescott. We would like whatever information you can give us about her son, adopted through a private agency sixteen years ago."

The judge looked at them both seriously for a few minutes. "Are you sure about this? Sometimes a little information isn't enough, and only whets the appetite for more. And that can't be given unless both sets of parents, birth and adoption, and the adult child are very sure they want it given. It's a big step," he added.

"It was a very big step for me to give him up," Maia said softly. "It was much bigger than I ever imagined it would be. And I truly believe, if I know Peter is well and...reasonably happy, I will be satisfied. I have never ever hoped to meet him. But," she added, "If you tell me he is not happy where he is, if I think I could make up to him for his unhappiness...then I'm not sure."

Judge Margerson studied her face for a long time before speaking. "Well, we'll cross that bridge when we come to it. For now, I believe I can arrange to give you basic information about Peter's situation if we have the records here."

"Your warm-hearted Miss Kittridge assured us the records are here," Andy said, then added, "She must discourage a lot of family reunions."

The judge smiled. "Yes, Miss Kittridge is a little...stern. She takes her responsibilities as guardian of the records very seriously. Check back with me next week. I believe we can have something for you by then."

They caught Dr. Sampson at the end of his office hours. His sparse gray hair was mussed and his pale blue eyes were tired. But his round face lit up when he saw Maia. "My dear girl!" and he embraced her. "Where have you been keeping yourself? I expected to see you around town this summer. You haven't even been at your job at the museum!" he added with mock seriousness.

Maia looked carefully into his face to see if there was any trace of accusation. "No, I've been...out of town. I took a little vacation, in a country house." It sounded so peaceful, Maia thought. Little vacation. Country house. How different from what it had become! *And how easy it is to dissemble,* she thought, *even without intent.*

"Well, what can I do for you? Sit down, sit down—and who is this young man?"

Andy ran his head over his graying hair and smiled at the description as Maia introduced him. She assured Dr. Sampson, on his query, that she was well, and this was not a medical call, then plunged into what she thought was the most difficult conversation she'd ever had.

"Dr. Sampson, I have to know...Mother's death...what was...what was the cause of death?"

The doctor stared at her in surprise. "Cause of death? You know the cause of death as well as I do! You lived with the cause of death for weeks. Your mother had cancer of the liver. She died of it. What kind of question is that?" he demanded gruffly, as if angry that she was wasting his time.

"Are you sure? Was there...anything...out of place...in Mother's room?"

"Why no! Your mother lay peacefully in her bed in final sleep. You were, as you know, in your bed. Your mother's friend, Ida Riker, had helped you. Seems you had a little fainting spell…"

"Yes, Ida Riker—she was there when I woke up." Maia was still confused.

"I think, my dear, your house in the country was too peaceful—gave you too much time to grieve and worry about nothing. I think you'd better move back to town and pick up your life again. Get back to work! Best cure for grief I know!" And he pushed from his desk and stood, excusing them.

He doesn't know, Maia thought. *He doesn't know! Ida knows! Ida was there first.*

Chapter 19

IDA RIKER WAS OUT OF TOWN for a week, visiting a daughter in Arkansas. That week, before Maia could talk with Ida, and before they could expect information from Judge Margerson's office, dragged interminably. Andy, who had begun to fill her life in a way she never knew was possible, was involved in a major drug investigation, and was rarely in the area.

Maia drove slowly back to Doria, arriving in late afternoon. After unloading a few groceries, she wandered around the house, hearing her soft-soled shoes whisper on the white marble floors, missing the click of Kastor's claws. She ran her fingers lightly over the bright blue arras she had hung on the white wall, marveling again at how it could be so soft when the sheep from which it came had such a rough life in the rugged Greek hills.

She pushed open the screen door, stood on the broad steps, and looked over the valley, where the sun painted a kaleidoscope of undulating autumn colors over the treetops—like, she thought, an ocean of psychedelic waves frozen to stillness. She wandered aimlessly down the hill, through the tall grasses, already tipped with delicate seeds and browning leaves. Small saplings had impinged further up the grassy knoll, recapturing inch by stubborn inch the area so painstakingly cleared by Philo Thad-something and his gardener. The goats, she thought…I should have gotten some goats to keep this area clear.

As she turned to go back up the hill, the sun caught the pillars of Doria in its receding rays and laid their shadows back against the house. Maia was back again, back to her first day at Doria when, walking up the hill from the shack, she had been struck with particular poignancy by Doria's resemblance to the Parthenon. And with that memory came the pain it had all brought—the sharp sadness she had tried to lose at the foot of those ancient Doric pillars and the still-fresh hurt of her mother's death. So much had happened since that afternoon—long hikes with Kastor, pleasure in knowing Herman, and Doria's beauty and solitude. And now all she had left was the solitude.

She resolutely closed her mind to sadness, looked from the white pillars down to the ground for sure footing in the grass and small trees, and plodded back up the hills.

As the light faded after supper, she decided a fire would brighten her spirits. The strange statue still guarded the woodpile, but it had lost its threatening aspect. It had become a benign symbol of Doria's particular and unusual ambience. No black-and-white cat slid from among the pines to startle Maia. She fell asleep in front of the dying fire, and no gray cat scratched at the window to waken her in a clutch of panic. She awoke in her chair in the morning, stiff and logy.

"This just won't do," she said aloud, forgetting again there was no Kastor to perk up his ears in agreement with whatever she said. "I guess I'll go back to Pembroke and wait out the week there. I should do something about Mother's house—the neighbors won't want to take care of it forever..." Her voice trailed off into the silence of the white walls and floors.

She drove away from Doria that morning with a heavy sense of melancholy. She had come there with such hopes of forgetting her hurts and beginning a new, brighter chapter of her life. But she had learned she couldn't do it alone. When Andy had been with her the past few months, Doria had been a happy place, full of pleasure and optimism for the future. But when she was alone, Doria was a constant reminder of all she had lost.

Maia opened her mother's house, freshened her old bed, bought a few groceries, and stayed in town. The closed house held the same stuffy air that had driven Maia away before. She visited the museum and agreed to think about coming back to work. She checked at the neighbor's on Sissy, the cat, who seemed neither unhappy nor elated to see her, but rubbed familiarly against her legs, reminding her unwillingly of the cats at Doria.

She went over, again and again, the last weeks of her mother's life. They circled in her brain like a carousel with discordant music...rounds of medications, nausea, pain, turning the frail body, pain, pain, pain. And the thoughts always came back to the moment with the pillow. Maia did not sleep much that week.

Andy made a point to be with her when it was time to go to the judge's office. He smiled broadly when they entered.

"I think you can relax about your son, Maia. We did an informal check on him, and found he is healthy, doing very well in school, takes part in school activities—captain of the debate team, in fact! He has a sister, two years his junior, born to his adoptive parents. So you see, he brought them good luck! The family seems to be functioning well, no obvious financial or other problems."

"Is his name...still Peter?" It was the only thing she had given him.

"I can't tell you that, Maia. I'm sorry. I've told you all I can."

"Would he...would he like to see me, do you think?"

"We assume he knows he is adopted, but we have no idea whether he would want to see you. When a child is happy and secure in a family, it seems a risk to introduce the birth parent.

When he is of age, eighteen, the question might be posed to him, and he could decide, then, with his adoptive parents."

Maia was satisfied. It would be wonderful to see him! And perhaps in a few years—not so long, compared with how long it had been.

Ida was home when Maia called the next day. Andy was out of town again, and Maia decided to visit Ida alone. Her house was just a block from Maia's mother's. Ida sat on the front porch, fanning herself in the autumn heat. She held Maia close a long time before releasing her.

"How are you, my dear? I've missed you! How did your summer go in that remote place in the hills? You never even called me!"

"I'm sorry, Ida. I didn't call anyone. I just had to get away…from…mother's house…from memories."

"Oh, I know how hard it has been for you. We all miss your mother, but can't wish her back, to her suffering. Come, sit down. I'm just having a cool drink—how does lemonade sound?

Maia smiled her thanks. "It sounds perfect for a hot afternoon on the front porch."

After Ida returned with another sweating glass, and they both settled themselves on a shabby but comfortable couch, Maia continued. "Ida…I have to talk with you. I just have to know about…Mother's death…what happened that day. I…can't…remember…"

Ida looked at her for a long moment before answering. "My dear, this has all been very hard for you. Are you sure you want to dredge it all up again?"

"It won't be 'dredged up,' Ida. That day has been in my mind for months! It's just that I don't know…exactly, what happened. And I think maybe the only way I'll be able to move on is to find that out."

"Well, I don't know exactly what happened either, dear. But I'll tell you what I do know. You have a right to relieve your mind as much as possible." She paused, closed her eyes as if to put herself back in time. "I came by late that afternoon to say hello to Helen. I knew she was very low, I didn't know how many more chances I would have to…see her."

"She was so miserable!"

"I know, I know. Anyway, no one answered when I knocked at the back door, so I let myself in with the key you gave me last winter. I called out to you, but you didn't answer, so I went on upstairs. Helen's door was open, the shades were drawn, it was shadowy and quiet. Helen was lying, quite still, her eyes half open, the way she often lay those past weeks after taking pain medication. I said her name a few times, but she didn't answer.

"Then when I stepped around to the other side of the bed, to put my hand on her forehead, to let her know I was there, there you were, on the floor by the bed! You seemed to have fainted or something, because you were unconscious. I left you there and called Dr. Sampson. His nurse said he'd come as fast as he could—and then I helped you to your own bed. You were in some kind of a state of shock, because you sort of stumbled along with me, but didn't seem to know what was going on. You didn't respond to your name. You didn't really waken until Dr. Sampson came. He…checked your mother first and told me she was…gone. Then we came to your room, and about that moment you tried to sit up. I guess you know the rest…"

Maia sat quietly, then asked softly, "What did he say…about Mother?"

"Just that the end had seemed to come peacefully, that he had been expecting it every day for a month."

"And…the pillow? What about the pillow?"

Ida's face tensed. "The pillow?"

"Yes, Mother's pillow that she always kept on her bed…where was it?"

Again Ida hesitated. "It was…under your hand…on the floor…beside you."

"Then you don't know…if…why I was…why it was on the floor by me?"

"No, dear, I don't know." She paused as if searching for a thought—or just the right words to express a thought. "Maybe you were going to prop up your mother's head… and when you realized she had passed away, you fainted, and the pillow fell with you."

"Or...maybe...I...held it over...maybe I killed her! Oh, Ida, she was in so much pain! Maybe I...you are the only person in the world I can ask! And I have to know!"

"I'm sorry, dear, I can't tell you. I...don't know. But the idea must have occurred to you, just as it occurred to me many times over the last few weeks of your mother's life. I just never had the courage to help ease the pain of my dearest friend!" Her voice turned ragged with emotion.

"I guess I'll have to live with...not knowing. It will be hard."

"But maybe not as hard as living with...knowing...," Ida said softly.

They looked long and deep into each other's eyes. Maia didn't ask any more.

Chapter 20

APRIL AGAIN. Maia sat on the patio of Doria, the sun warming her shoulders. The lightest tinge of delicate green was spreading over the bare branches in the valley. The thawing ground emanated the earthy aroma of fertility. Winter birds, sparrows and chickadees, darted among the evergreens, flitting shadows deep in the shadowy reaches of pine needles and branches, chirping their short, sweet promises of spring. Maia wondered how she could ever have thought April cruel.

She looked down to where the trees, mixed with fir, pine, and spruce, were thick enough even without leaves to hide the roofs of The Place. She still shrank within herself when she thought of all that had been going on so near her home, without her having any suspicion. How little we really know—of anyone and anything, no matter how close, she thought.

The Place was changing now. The general store had been sold to a young couple who were trying to repair, paint, and tidy it up. Maia admired their hard work and optimism. The store had almost seemed a changeless moment to the character of The Place—but she was sorry they were changing the product line: the feta cheese and black oily, salty olives had been replaced by American brick and kosher dills. The heavy crusty bread Selena had occasionally baked no longer lay in lumpy, uneven loaves, sending their yeasty aroma up the aisles. Instead, the bread racks held light, sliced, doughy versions, firmly wrapped in plastic bags, sitting primly and uniformly side by side.

The counters were gradually being neatened, and an orderly, rational display of merchandise was replacing the jumble of odds and ends Selena had so proudly claimed as necessary to life. Maia wondered if the community would be as well served.

Her eyes wandered to the copse of trees where Herman had "come home" to spread out his grimy sleeping bag and play his little flute. Without knowing she did so, Maia listened for those sweet notes to come gently up the hill. But no more, ever. The shack was gone, with Doria's owner's permission, taken down in one afternoon of clouds of dust, crashing boards, and nails shrieking as they resisted being wrenched from timbers they had held for decades. Maia had stayed inside Doria, doors firmly closed, and would not look as Andy and a worker from The Place hauled the debris up the hill and loaded it into an old truck. She hadn't gone down since to the spot where the shack had stood. Maybe some day. But she had wondered where the feral cats had gone. Were they frightened away by the racket of demolition? Or had they left when Herman left?

One warm day, though, she had found her way to the clearing where the big, flat stone still stood like a primitive altar in the center. The long grasses had turned brown and lay crisp and tangled all around. The spot where Kastor was buried was hardly distinguishable except that the spade Phiny had used still stood upright where he had plunged it. The reality of the spade and what it stood for, and the hulking, hard permanence of the rock helped Maia dispense once and for all the lingering tentative emotions for Phiny she still occasionally felt. She realized she never would know exactly what had happened that strange, hot day in June. She had listened to reports of Phiny's indictment, trial, and subsequent sentence of a long prison term with stoic calmness. She would let herself feel neither regret that she would never again know the giddy exhilaration nor the anger that she had been used by him. She would put it all behind her.

She had a great deal with which to replace it. Maia breathed in the beauty of the day again, looked down, and touched the most beautiful thing of all—the perfect little head covered with black, silky hair. Peter stirred, and his tiny hands fluttered toward his face. He took a deep quivering breath, and settled back into calm sleep. Maia's body could hardly contain her heart, she was so happy. And she could hardly believe her life. Peter, this tiny three-month-old Peter, was hers—hers and Andy's! In spite of her best efforts to persuade Canthy to keep him, he was hers!

Maia looked down again over the trees that hid the roofs of The Place and remembered how she had pleaded with Canthy, promised every kind of support within her powers—her company, financial, emotional—if Canthy would only keep her baby. They had sat in the tiny, dilapidated cottage all through the beautiful autumn days, while leaves turned nature's palette flamboyant with reds, oranges, and gold. And they had argued.

Canthy had been very sick the first months of her pregnancy, before Maia even knew of it. Those miserable days and nights, combined with Canthy's fury about Herman's abandoning her, gave her a deep and abiding distaste for the baby she carried. She sat morosely while Maia explained that these memories and resentments would pass—that when she saw her baby she would forget the bad times, that she would just know she had to keep her child safe and near. Maia even shared the pain yet again of her own regrets and heartaches because she had made the decision Canthy seemed determined to make herself. But Canthy resisted every argument.

Selena was not much help. Her one venture into motherhood had not been highly satisfactory. Instead of encouraging Canthy to keep her baby, she sat placidly by while Maia pleaded. Maia guessed Selena figured she would be the practicing parent if Canthy kept the baby, and she was not very enthused about the prospect.

And Selena was worried about Barney. His indictment, trial, and sentencing were moving along inexorably. In spite of his grim facade and questionable choice of career, Barney had evoked a fierce loyalty in Selena. When he was sentenced to five years in prison in a southern state, Selena opted to move to be near him as soon as her probation for her part in the drug ring was over. Canthy saw that move as her chance to see new places, find new excitement, and escape the harsh Maine winters for warmer climes. She wanted to go with her mother. And a baby would cramp her style!

Maia had, with Andy's "real estate" connections, extended her lease of Doria, with an option to buy. He had also helped her sell her mother's house. She agreed to go back to work at the museum part-time over the winter months, determined that the long drive would not be too hard.

And, between his long and frequent absences, Andy continued to court Maia. He confided that he'd been married briefly several years before. The marriage had ended in a mutually agreeable divorce, partially because of his wife's reluctance to have children. He had then become so involved in his work he hadn't had time to develop a lasting relationship with anyone—until Maia had called him about Doria.

"That call was the beginning, honey," he said. "It became abundantly clear early on that you were going to be lonely up here—in spite of living very close to that festering circle of druggies. I just hoped you wouldn't get involved. That's why I kept doing 'appraisals' up here!"

"Your interest was certainly not appreciated at the time," Maia laughed. "You always showed up at the most inopportune time! Except that last time!" she added hastily.

They were married at Christmas, in Judge Margerson's chambers. Ida Riker was Maia's attendant, and the judge's wife was the other witness. They moved their belongings to Doria to start the new year together.

Maia and Andy were both concerned about Canthy's baby, and when it became official that she was putting it up for adoption, Judge Margerson helped them through the bureaucratic jungle to assure them they would be the adoptive parents.

The baby was born in January, a six-pound boy. Maia visited Canthy and asked again if she wanted to keep him.

"How can you not want to keep him?" she asked desperately.

"I don't want him," was all Canthy would say as she turned her face to the wall.

This fine April day was Peter's first outing at Doria. Maia wanted him to breathe the still air, clear today of the wood-processing odors, and feel the warm sun. So she had moved his bassinet onto the patio for his afternoon nap. As time for another bottle approached, the baby stirred, opened his dark blue eyes, and focused them on Maia's face. A baby smile melted her heart.

She handed him the only toy he seemed to like—Herman's little flute that Maia had found in the shack. She had scrubbed it clean and offered it to Peter when he was first able to grasp anything. He had immediately put one end into his mouth. "Wrong end, precious!" Maia had laughed, and had tried to take it form him, but he had screamed his objection lustily in his strangely hoarse voice.

As he moved his arms, waving the flute in a tiny ball of fist, and kicked off the light fluffy quilt, Maia saw again his little bare feet, severely deformed. Maia tried not to remember her sharp shock when she had first seen those tiny feet. She did not want to think of the Greek god Pan, son of Hermes: Pan, god of forests, Pan, with goat feet. Peter was perfect except for his feet. Andy and Maia had been assured that corrective surgery would enable Peter to walk and run normally. But it couldn't be done for many months, and would have to be repeated as he grew.

Maia was grateful, again and for this new reason, that Canthy had given Peter up, as Maia knew Canthy would never have the resources, financial or emotional, to have the surgeries done. She and Andy would be privileged to help this beautiful child to a normal life.

As Peter kicked and cooed and waved his flute, Maia became aware of movement behind her—and to the side. Her eyes widened. The cats! It was the feral cats, back again! The tiger striped, the black and white, the big gray—they were back! They crept silently across the patio and rubbed against the bassinet, tails twitching, purring and making soft meowing sounds. Peter smiled again as the big gray cat lifted its head and looked directly into his eyes.

Maia looked up at the tall pillars of Doria, their shadows like bars against the walls, and knew, willing or unwilling, she was their prisoner.

To order additional copies of this book,
please send full amount plus $4.00 for
postage and handling for the first book and
50¢ for each additional book.

Send orders to:

Galde Press, Inc.
PO Box 460
Lakeville, Minnesota 55044-0460

Credit card orders call 1–800–777–3454
Phone (612) 891–5991 • Fax (612) 891–6091
Visit our website at http://www.galdepress.com

Write for our free catalog.

NORMANDALE COMMUNITY COLLEGE
LIBRARY
9700 FRANCE AVENUE SOUTH
BLOOMINGTON, MN 55431-4399